COFFIN SHADOWS

COFFIN SHADOWS

Glen Krisch & Mark Steensland

CEMETERY DANCE PUBLICATIONS

Baltimore

❖ 2023 ❖

Cemetery Dance Publications
132B Industry Lane, Unit #7
Forest Hill, MD 21050
www.cemeterydance.com

Trade Paperback Edition

ISBN:
978-1-58767-864-6

Cover Artwork and Design © 2023 by Luke Spooner
Cover and Interior Design © 2023 by Desert Isle Design, LLC

CHAPTER 1

1.

San Francisco, Early October

JANET AND BRIAN walked along the waterfront, holding hands while browsing the vendor tables at the Ferry Plaza Farmers' Market. Her fiancé didn't normally care if their produce was fresh or not, locally-sourced organic or flown in from the other side of the world. But he liked spending time with her, and she liked that he made the effort. At any rate, they both enjoyed the meals they prepared together, falling into an easy, familiar dance as they moved about the kitchen. That's how she saw their relationship—the easy dance of two people who cared deeply for one another.

She squeezed Brian's hand when a display of purple fingerling potatoes caught her eye.

"Hold on a second." Janet stopped, picked up a potato, rolled it in her palm. She was picturing a garlicy potato soup, perhaps a side salad. Yes, perfect!

"I'll take two pints," she said to the vendor.

"Good choice," the old man said.

Brian shifted impatiently from foot to foot until his phone buzzed in his pocket. He pulled it out and checked his texts while the farmer filled Janet's canvas bag with produce.

"Thank you," she said as she pocketed her change.

Brian couldn't hide his goofy grin when she turned toward him.

"What?" she said, feeling uncertain. "What was the message?"

"Nothing." His smile only widened. "Don't worry about it." He took hold of her hand again as they started back down the aisle.

Oh great. A surprise. She sighed. Janet hated surprises, and Brian didn't seem to understand it yet. But what could it be? A surprise party? Her birthday was three months away, so that couldn't be it. He wouldn't have that silly expression over a simple flower or candy delivery. The only time he'd ever looked like that was when he mentioned getting a puppy together, a month earlier.

He didn't get a puppy without me knowing, did he? she thought. Please don't let it be a puppy!

As they drifted between the booths, a flash of movement caught the corner of her eye.

A boy in a red rain coat darted across the aisle, then hid behind a tree trunk.

"What is it?" Brian said, taking hold of her hand.

They stepped closer to the tree, and the boy, with much of his face obscured by his hood, peeked out at her. She saw his eyes, clearly, and he was obviously staring at her. A light blue or gray, she thought, wanting to see him up close. He looked familiar. His size. His age.

Brian gently squeezed her fingers. "Honey?"

The boy didn't move, but she sensed tension in his posture, like a bowstring pulled taut, readying to fire an arrow.

Janet pulled away from Brian's touch and trotted over to the tree trunk. When she circled around it, no one was near, nor did she see anything red that would confuse her about his rain coat.

"Okay, you're starting to scare me a little," Brian said with a forced laugh when he reached her side.

"It's just...I thought I saw..." she trailed off, puzzled. "Never mind. It was nothing."

"Are you sure? Because you looked spooked. Still do, in fact."

"I'm fine. Can we just go?"

"Yeah. Sure."

During the whole walk back to the car, Brian tried to bring her back to her good mood, but she wasn't up for it. She kept her eyes panning the milling people, looking for that boy.

2.

BRIAN TURNED his Mazda onto their street in the Mission District. They shared a two-bedroom apartment in a rambling old Victorian. Others might have seen it as a money pit, but when they first saw it at the beginning of the summer—with the surrounding neighborhood's eclectic mix of creatives, educators, and tech entrepreneurs—they knew they'd found the perfect home to start their life together.

Brian's goofy grin returned, and widened even, when he spotted a parking space only a block from the apartment. "Hey, look at that!"

"It's a minor miracle!" Janet said as he pulled into the spot.

When they left the car, they had to navigate around a man wearing an expensive suit squatting down to clean up after his Goldendoodle. He was using a plastic grocery bag like a protective glove, and the dog looked happy about the arrangement.

Janet didn't want to have to walk a dog outside in all types of weather. She wondered if Brian might compromise and agree to getting a cat.

As they walked up the steps to their apartment, he said, "Close your eyes."

"You're kidding, right?" Janet pictured little puddles of puppy pee, sharp-pitched cries in the middle of the night. He motioned for her to close her eyes. "This is silly."

Brian chuckled. "It is not. And no peeking."

She closed her eyes, feeling tense. "What if I trip?"

"I'll catch you, of course."

Her heart fluttered. *Of course, you would.*

With a hand on the small of her back, he guided her.

"Okay, step," he said.

She inched her foot up the step leading to the door of their ground floor apartment.

"Step."

She complied, even though she felt like she was being drawn into a trap. Dogs lived, what…ten years? Fifteen? That was such a long commitment. And they'd only recently moved in together.

"Okay, last one."

She climbed the last step and waited as he unlocked the door.

"Okay, take my hand," he said.

His hand was sweaty. Yet, she didn't hear the telltale whine of a puppy.

Brian walked in front of her as he led her down the hallway. They stopped at the doorway to the home office. Brian took a deep breath.

"Can I look now?" Janet asked, starting to feel nervous.

"Not until I turn the light on." He flipped the switch. "Go ahead."

When she opened her eyes, she saw a baby crib with a big bow around it. "This is it? The big surprise?" Her whole spirit deflated. "I shouldn't have told you," she said, unable to rein in the pain from her voice.

"It's mine, too, you know," he said, each syllable quieter than the previous.

"Not right now, it isn't." Her hand went to her belly. She wasn't even showing yet. This was way too early, and from out of nowhere.

Janet pushed past him, across the hallway and into the bathroom. She closed the door firmly, then heard the soft tread as Brian followed. He stopped right outside the door. She placed her palm against white faux wood, shook her head. He raised his hand to knock—she could feel it—before lowering it. Without a word, he walked away.

3.

ABOUT AN hour later, Janet felt composed enough for the fight that would likely end them. When she came out of the bathroom, the door to the office was closed. Brian had made fried chicken and mashed the purple potatoes she'd bought at the farmer's market.

Brian turned away from the stove as she approached. He gave her a slight nod and brought a serving dish with steamed asparagus to the table set for two.

He sighed heavily before meeting her eye. "I'm sorry. Okay?"

"Me, too." There were so many layers to those two brief words, but she didn't feel up to sorting it all out.

"I guess I just don't understand."

She felt a flash of sympathy for his confusion, but only a flash. "I know you don't."

"Maybe if you explained it to me."

"Maybe if I thought you'd listen."

"That's not fair."

"But surprising me with a crib is?"

"I wasn't thinking. I'm sorry."

"The more you say that, the less I believe you."

"What should I say?" Brian leaned forward with his palms on the back of a dining chair.

"That you love me and you'll respect my decision, whatever it is."

"I do. And I will."

Janet exhaled a deep, steadying breath before taking her seat. They ate in near silence. Janet finally offered an olive branch when she complimented the potatoes. "I was thinking a soup, but these are delicious."

Brian smiled sheepishly.

No sudden moves… If there aren't any sudden moves, Janet thought as she scooped more potatoes onto her fork, we might just be okay. As long as no one drops the nitroglycerin topic of their baby.

No, my baby.

CHAPTER 2

I.

JANET LET THE hot shower spray waken her slowly. She'd had trouble sleeping, so she woke up groggy, in a fog. It was surreal how life went on. Since today was a Monday, she had a full week of teaching ahead of her. No matter what happened last night, a new day would always dawn.

A thought solidified, bringing her fully awake. It almost ended last night. Her eyes opened fully, then widened. Me and Brian. Just...done.

But he'd smiled at the end of dinner, at least a little bit, and they'd worked together—sure, nearly wordlessly, but still together—to clear the table and wash the dishes. She hoped they would be okay. She'd never been in a better relationship.

Time. That's all they needed. Well, that and understanding. Perhaps, from both of them.

After her shower, she got dressed and went into the kitchen. The sink was empty, spotless. She gathered frozen berries, protein powder, and Greek yogurt and blended up a smoothie. She sipped on her last-minute breakfast and went into the bedroom to get her jacket.

The bed was not only empty, but made. She furrowed her brow, poked her head into the bathroom. Also empty.

After grabbing a light tan jacket from the closet, she went out to the hallway, listening. She heard the metallic clanking of hand tools—a wrench turned, clumsily, around a nut. An exasperated sigh.

Janet followed the sound and opened the door to the office. Brian looked up, dressed in pajama pants and a faded concert T, his hair sticking up in sleep horns. He held an adjustable wrench, had already taken apart half the crib. Unassembled pieces fanned out around him.

"I didn't know you were awake," she said.

"I heard the shower. Thought I'd get a jump on things so I can return it on my way to work." He tilted his head, his eyes narrowing. "Unless you don't want me to."

"For now, it's for the best." She held the smoothie out to him, no longer hungry. "Want the rest of this?"

"Does it have kale in it?" He curled his lip at the thought.

Janet shook her head and handed him the smoothie cup. He sipped it and nodded his approval. She kissed him.

"Don't forget to rinse that before you put it in the dishwasher."

"You just tricked me into doing your dishes again, didn't you?"

"You got me. I love you." Her laughter, quite welcome in the given circumstances, carried her to the door as she shouldered her backpack. And she meant it. She loved him, felt so very in love with him, even still.

"Love you, too," he replied.

Was that the slightest hesitation on his part?

2.

JANET WALKED her bike out onto the front step and closed the door behind her. The air was cool with humidity blown in off the bay on a gentle breeze. Perfect for her morning commute. After adjusting her helmet, she walked her bike down the steps, climbed on, and pedaled away.

The hill sloped downward, gently at first, then as she reached the next block, the elevation really dropped off, allowing her to pick up speed with ease. The Mission spread out before her, an artistic, intricate, and sometimes thriving neighborhood she and Brian adored. Every stretch of road, every hill of her route to work, was as familiar to her as the back of her hand. She shifted into low gear as she attacked a steep incline. Concentrating on the rhythmic motions of the climb helped to push back against the thoughts of tension between her and Brian. She pedaled harder, leaning over the handlebars.

Two miles later, Janet turned into the fenced playground at Earlyside Elementary and coasted to a stop at the side door all the teachers used. The staff parking lot was already packed. She could hear children's laughter and excited chatter from around the corner of the building. Buses disgorging students, parents in minivans snaking along the drop-off lane.

She removed her helmet and shook out her hair before shouldering her bike to take inside. The school hummed with the kinetic vibe of early morning. It was the short window of time when the kids were awake and the teachers were still buzzing from their morning coffees. She rolled the bike down the corridor and into the teachers' lounge.

"Cutting it kind of close, huh, Janet?" Harold Daubens, the music teacher, said as he bit into a doughnut glazed in hot pink frosting. He glanced at the clock on the wall, raised an eyebrow.

"It's still half an hour before first bell. That's plenty of time!" She ran her fingers through her hair, still feeling the calm brought on by her ride through town.

"I don't know how you do it," Harold said.

"Do what?"

"Not let the world weigh you down." He took another bite, and jelly dribbled onto his tie. "Ah, there I go again." He stuffed the last of the doughnut into his mouth to free his hands. He went to the sink and wiped at his tie with a damp rag.

"It's all projection, because that's certainly not how I feel on the inside."

"So, how does it feel, Ms. Martlee, on the inside…" someone said from the doorway, "to let your coworkers down?"

Janet turned at the pinched voice to see Principal Merriwether, dressed, as usual, in a gray cardigan over a drab black dress. Janet wondered again how long it took the woman to pull her hair into a bun that tight. And what did she think those pearls added? Respectability? Maybe. She was no taller than some of the children at Earlyside and this no doubt contributed to her overcompensation in temperament. She was as cold and severe as fluffy snow packed into a rock-hard ball.

"I'm sorry?" Janet said, not following.

"Did you forget again?"

"Do I have yard duty?" Janet asked, feeling a surge of panic.

"No. You're on the crosswalk this morning. Supposed to be, anyway. Angela's down there now."

Of course, she had to forget crosswalk duty. And poor Angela would be covering for her. That intersection could be a total madhouse at this time of morning.

"Sorry! I completely forgot."

"Of course you did. You better get moving."

"Right!" Janet hung her bike helmet on the handlebars.

As she passed Principal Merriwether, the little woman waved her through the doorway, chanting, "Go on, go on!"

3.

"ANGELA, I'M so sorry!" Janet said as she jogged out to meet her friend.

Angela smirked, accentuating her high cheekbones. She held a stop sign as she waited for the next gaggle of kids to approach the crosswalk from the surrounding neighborhood. She wore her jet-black hair in a super-cute pixie cut. She wore stylish clothes, and her face looked serene, as if she were enjoying a day at Muir Beach. Angela was her best friend; Janet could count on her for anything. And here Janet was, once again, letting her down.

"I'm the least of your worries." Angela turned and motioned surreptitiously to the second-floor window behind her.

Janet glanced over her shoulder. Principal Merriwether stared down at them. Is she sneering at me?

"No kidding," Janet said. "God, I miss Holly."

"Me, too. Who told her she could get pregnant, right?" Angela removed her reflective vest and handed it over to Janet.

"So true. Did she ask us before she decided to take that monumental leap?" Janet pulled on the vest and took the stop sign from Angela.

"I know, right?" Angela pointed at Janet's belly. She'd only told her friend about her own pregnancy a few days ago. "Like, maybe, it would be something to talk about ahead of time?"

Janet had thought about not telling Angela, in case she decided to not keep the baby, but she hadn't been able to keep the secret. She'd halfway expected her friend to shame her, but in the end, of course Angela had been super supportive.

"What's your excuse this time?" Angela said playfully.

"I forgot," Janet said, and it sounded even more lame than in her head.

"Please. I need something more dramatic than that."

"There's a hostage situation at Mission Dolores. The police have ten blocks closed in every direction."

Angela walked out to the sidewalk. "Ah, that's too dramatic."

"Well, the truth is what it is," Janet said, taking up her position in the crosswalk. "I forgot. Like I always forget. I don't know how you put up with me."

One mother at the street corner held a little boy's hand. She shouted, "Can we cross, please?"

"I better go." Angela waved to Janet.

"I'll make it up to you. Promise."

"I know you will." Angela shook her head as she hurried to the doorway.

A car honked, and Janet glared at the driver. The driver, embarrassed, pretended to check the radio dial. Janet waved the group of students and parents across.

"Good morning, Miss Martlee," a girl said as she passed.

"Good morning, Charlotte. I like your dress!"

"Thank you!" Charlotte said. "I like your smile!"

Oh, these kids are the best, she thought.

When the group reached the other side of the road, Janet was ready to let the traffic go. Before she did, she noticed a boy in a dark red jacket on the far side, standing with his back to her.

Another driver honked and she gave him an irritated look. When she looked at the corner again, the boy was gone. Nowhere to be found.

She lowered her stop sign and waved the drivers through.

The driver of the first car to gun past her flashed her his middle finger. She ignored it. She continued to look for the boy in the red jacket as traffic zoomed by.

Did he walk away?

Why would he do that?

It's almost time for first bell.

Then she saw him. He was standing near the bus stop bench, staring at her. His lips broke into an impish grin, then widened as he lifted a hand to wave to her.

At first, she thought his eyes were light blue. Then she realized they were gray and rheumy…diseased.

Not diseased, she thought. Dead.

A car horn blared, and she whipped her head around. A pickup truck zoomed by, inches from her hip.

When she turned back, the boy in the red jacket stepped into traffic. He was staring at her still, those dead gray eyes searching. Pleading.

A silver sedan accelerated toward him, and her heart stammered in her chest.

"No!" she shouted and charged forward, hoping to get close enough to pull him to safety. She waved her stop sign, but the silver sedan didn't seem to notice her.

Until it was too late.

The car's bumper slammed into the boy, and he went under its wheels. The thump and trundle of flesh pulped by steel was sickening.

Janet stepped in front of the car, arms braced for impact. Luckily, the sedan came to a complete stop just short of her trembling legs.

"Hey, lady, are you crazy?" the driver, a man with a mustache waxed into curls, shouted out the window.

"The boy!" she seethed. "You hit that boy!"

"What are you talking about?" The man shifted into park and got out, coming around to the front.

Janet didn't want to see the damage, the blood and viscera painting the silver bumper.

She looked down.

"What boy?" The man stood with his hands on his hips, his anger unmistakable.

"I-I don't…" she stuttered. She got on her hands and knees. Saw nothing staining the street but globs of blackened bubblegum and streaks of oil.

"You need to get your head examined."

"I…" She looked around at the people on the sidewalks gaping at her. "I'm sorry, sir. I just thought… I thought I saw…"

"You're lucky I'm late for work or I'd be dragging your ass inside to tell your boss."

The man climbed back into his car, slammed the door, and pulled away in a rush.

Traffic resumed within seconds as if nothing had happened. Because nothing had happened. There was no boy splattered on the pavement. No blood. No gore. No sign the boy had been there to begin with.

But he was there. I saw him. He grinned at me! I heard his body smashed into the asphalt.

"Should we cross?" a mother said at the crosswalk. The woman looked concerned, but not concerned enough to offer to help.

The thud and squelch of the car running the boy over echoed through her mind.

"Yes. Sorry about that!" Janet jogged over and held up her stop sign. The tide of people crossed. The signals changed. Traffic flowed from the other direction. Within a couple of minutes, the last witnesses to her embarrassment were long gone, thankfully.

A few minutes before first bell, she finally put the boy out of mind and left the crosswalk. As she made her way to the school's front steps, she noticed Principal Merriwether watching from the second-floor window.

1.

THE LOW hum of her students' whispered conversations filled the classroom as Janet walked between the desks, handing papers to her two-dozen second graders. An animated cloud filled the paper, and a question floated above the cloud: "WHAT DO YOU SEE?"

When she made sure each of her students had a copy, she returned to the front of the room. She said, "And how many of you have played a game like this before?"

Everyone raised their hands.

"Okay," she said with a chuckle, buoyed by their enthusiasm. "Good. This is basically the same thing, except you'll be making the cloud into what you see. This project is all about your imaginations. What you see when you close your eyes."

She noticed Saber pick up a crayon, ready to start.

"Don't start drawing right away," she said, staring at the boy.

Disappointed, he put the crayon down.

"Spend a few minutes with your imagination. Let it tell you what the cloud looks like. Everybody understand?"

"Yes, Miss Martlee," the class replied in a ruffled chorus.

Janet put the leftover papers on her desk, then went to the wall where she had hung a banner that said: "THE POWER OF IMAGINATION."

"And when you're all done," she continued, "we'll put them up here for everyone to see at next week's Open House."

The hum of conversation intensified as her students set about the task. Janet sat at her desk, keeping an eye on the students. Some of the kids had indeed listened to her and were now staring off into space, in deep thought. Others, anxious to get the work done no matter how slapdash, were a flurry of drawing and coloring.

Her kids were such a microcosm of humans in general. At that tender age you could try your hardest to shape and guide them so they worked diligently, followed the rules, and completed tasks on time, but the longer she was an elementary school teacher, the more she thought those propensities were traits you were born with.

When the bell rang, she gathered the class into a single file and they headed down the hallway toward the library. She glanced back, and for the most part, the kids followed her strides with quiet focus. She always felt like a mama duck with her ducklings toddling behind.

She smiled at the thought as they reached the glass double doors outside the library.

Mrs. B., a woman in her sixties who treated the library as her own personal domain, stood at the doorway.

"Hello, Mrs. B." Janet knew her surname, which was Bartowski, but since all the kids called her by the abbreviation, she did also. While she did this for consistency's sake, it made her feel somewhat inferior to the librarian.

Mrs. B. barred the way, standing in front of the double doors. "Miss Martlee," she said, but her gaze was on the children, and under the intensity of her gaze the second graders stood more upright. A couple of boys re-straightened their line.

"All right boys and girls, as soon as you're completely quiet, we'll go in." Janet waited.

Finally, after making them stand at attention for a half minute longer than necessary, Mrs. B. said, "All right everyone, you may enter." She waved them forward, and the class pressed through the doors in single file before they scattered in all directions once they crossed into the quiet sanctum of the library.

Mrs. B. finally looked at Janet. "10:15, please."

"Of course. 10:15, sharp."

Mrs. B. checked her wristwatch and clucked her tongue as she followed in the children's wake.

5.

A FAT orange tabby named Moe sat on the stack of cloud drawings on Janet's desk. Mrs. Abernathy, a long-since retired teacher, began feeding the skinny stray when he was still young and spry. Now, Moe seemed as much a part of Earlyside as the green tile floor of the hallway. She shooed him off and took the drawings to the wall with the banner on it. She paused a few seconds with each picture, smiling as she stapled them to the board, chuckling at some, sighing proudly at others.

Moe meowed and pressed against her legs.

"Pretty good, aren't they?" she said.

She gazed at a sheep, an ice cream sundae, a mountain range—even a clown car… Janet stopped smiling. One of the children had transformed the cloud into a fanged demon with black hair and red eyes.

She flipped the picture over fast, searching for the student's name. Nothing.

When Janet looked at the demon face again, Moe growled—a low, guttural sound that rapidly became a hiss.

In the window, Janet saw the blurry reflection of a figure standing in the doorway behind her.

A red jacket? She knew immediately it was the boy from the crosswalk. The boy with the dead eyes and knowing grin. The drawing slipped from her fingers as she whirled on her heels.

Angela stood in the doorway.

"Whoa, sorry," Angela said, holding her hands up in apology. "I didn't mean to scare you."

"No, it wasn't you. Take a look at this drawing."

Angela approached the wall and pointed at the clown car. "I can see why. I hate clowns."

"Not that one," Janet said, bending down. The demonic drawing had fallen under a desk. She reached for it, snagged it with the tip of her index finger. "This one."

She handed it to Angela, who looked at it and shrugged.

"And I thought I was weird." Angela chuckled.

Janet took the drawing back, shocked to see it was no longer a demon but a cow with big brown spots. She flipped it over and saw Braden Pauley's scribbled name. She frowned.

Angela touched her shoulder. "I was only joking. I didn't know you're afraid of cows."

"I'm not," Janet replied. She couldn't stop staring at the silly drawing. How could I have mistaken…?

"But you said…"

Janet shook her head and sighed heavily. "I thought it was something else."

"Like what?"

"A face. A demon or something."

"Are you high?" Angela said, again chuckling, this time trying to lighten the mood.

"Joking again?"

Angela shrugged. "Trying."

"Try harder." Janet forced a smile.

"Ouch." Angela took the cow picture, looked at it a moment, then looked at Janet. "You don't think it could be because of, you know…?" She gestured to Janet's belly.

"No. It didn't happen before," she said, placing a hand on her belly. Is it already getting a bit round? Can't be. It's too early for that. "Last time, I got sick, but I didn't see things." Janet looked at the clock. "Oh, no! Gotta go. Bye!"

Angela smirked, used to Janet's time management issues.

Janet ran down the hallway. When she rounded the corner, her class was already lined up outside the library, waiting.

Principal Merriwether stood next to Mrs. B. They looked like the twins from The Shining, but grown up and full of bitterness.

As Janet slowed to a stop, Mrs. B. said with smug satisfaction, "I said 10:15, Miss Martlee."

"I know. I'm sorry," Janet said. "Moe got sick and I had to clean it up."

The class gave a collective "Eww!"

"Quiet, everyone," Principal Merriwether said.

"Tell Mrs. B. thank you, class."

"Thank you, Mrs. B.," they said as one.

Janet led them away.

6.

THE AIR was cool, the sky overcast. As Janet watched her class on the playground, she pictured buying Halloween decorations with Brian. Carving Jack-o'-lanterns for the front steps of their apartment.

But what if it doesn't work out? Will Brian and I even be together in another month?

Tears began to gather on her lower eyelids. She blinked and sniffed, trying her hardest to push the negative thoughts away.

She took in the sight of her kids—they really were her kids, at least for half the day—and smiled at their games of jump rope, freeze tag, and superheroes. They wore hats and coats against the cold. Janet stopped smiling when Ukiah approached her, crying softly.

"What's wrong, Ukiah?"

"Nobody will push me on the swings."

"Who'd you ask?" Janet looked out at the playground for someone so cruel to deny adorable Ukiah.

"Well...nobody."

"Hmm...how about I push you?"

Ukiah nodded and walked out to the swing set. Janet helped her onto a swing and gave her a push.

"Higher!" Ukiah said, her tears long gone.

"You don't want to go too high."

"Yes, I do. Higher!"

Janet laughed. But her happiness vanished as soon as she noticed the boy in the dark red jacket, standing with his back to the brick wall near the bathrooms. His hands were stuffed in his pockets, his head tilted low so she couldn't see his face. But it was him. She was certain.

"Keep pushing!" Ukiah said.

Janet snapped out of it long enough to give Ukiah another push.

When she looked toward the bathroom again, the boy was gone.

She pushed Ukiah again, her thoughts divided. Her eyes panned the playground, searching. She spotted him opening the classroom door and going inside. Janet stopped pushing Ukiah and blew her whistle.

"Recess is over," she said in her strong teacher voice. "Everyone line up."

The children playfully complained and begged for more time.

"I said line up right now!"

Her tone shocked them into silence. Janet herded them toward the classroom the boy had entered. She rushed them inside, making sure she had accounted for everyone, then hurried them down the hallway.

When she tried to open the door to her classroom, it was locked. That was unusual. She never locked it, just in case one of the students needed to return for something while they were outside. She used the key hanging on a lanyard around her neck and unlocked it.

A low hum rose from her class as Janet looked inside the room, but it was empty. She turned on the lights but still didn't see anyone.

"Okay. Everyone inside," she said, standing aside. "Hang up your hats and coats and take your seats."

The students filed in, doing as they were told. After the last student entered, Janet closed the door and locked it, then went to her desk. She picked up a small handbell and rang it until the students stopped talking and faced forward.

"Okay, everyone, get out your reading workbook." She set the bell down and then saw a pair of legs sticking out from under some of the jackets on the rack, as if someone were hiding inside them.

She glanced at the class. All the desks were occupied. "Open your workbook to page…" she said as she walked to the back of the room. She pushed the coats aside.

And stood face to face with the boy in the dark red jacket.

His face was ghastly blue. He blinked his clouded dead eyes.

"Help me..." the boy whispered, as if an obstruction filled his throat. His breath smelled of death. He smiled that knowing grin, his teeth broken shards impaling gray gums.

Janet screamed and stumbled away. She fell on her backside, tried crab-walking away. Her vision dimmed as her strength drained from her. The coats parted, and the boy stepped out from the shadows. She tried to scream again, but had no breath, and when she attempted to take in more air, the room spun and everything went dark.

CHAPTER 3

I.

JANET LAY ON a cot inside a curtained-off section of the nurse's office. She stared at the pinprick pattern of the ceiling tiles as if trying to decipher some hidden message. At least it no longer felt like the ceiling was spinning.

She sat up, stood unsteadily, and when her legs solidified beneath her, pushed the curtain aside. The nurse saw her and hurried over.

"Hold on, now. Take it easy." The nurse helped Janet sit down again.

"How did I get here?"

"They said you were holding a jacket in your hand, waving it around, screaming…" the nurse trailed off, met her gaze as if uncertain if she should continue.

"I was?" Janet rubbed her temples, stunned. She had flashes of memory from what had happened, but the more she concentrated, the more her head hurt. "Was there anything else? Did I say anything?"

"'I guess you were screaming, 'Get out. Leave me alone,' over and over," the nurse said with a frown.

"You guess?" Janet filled with panicked despair and her cheeks flushed with embarrassment. "Please tell me you didn't hear me clear across the school."

"No, it's just what I heard," the nurse said, looking away. She continued, almost whispering: "Mrs. Linsey in the classroom across the hall from you mentioned it. She wasn't gossiping, just…concerned. As we all are. You were calm by the time they got you in here. Nearly catatonic, I'd say. You told me you were tired and wanted to lie down. That was two hours ago."

"Okay...okay," Janet muttered, trying to make sense of things.

Maybe it's not so bad? she thought. Maybe I won't have to hide my head in shame every time I enter the building?

"Thank you for taking care of me." She smiled at the nurse. "I really appreciate it."

If the nurse is taking care of me—

Janet stood up with a jolt. "My class!"

The nurse placed a hand on her shoulder. Her touch was gentle, but she also seemed ready to take charge and guide Janet back onto the cot if need be. "Don't worry. They got a sub. I'll call Principal Merriwether. She wanted to see you when you woke up, anyway. Can I get you a glass of water?"

2.

PRINCIPAL MERRIWETHER sat behind her desk, while Janet sat across from her, waiting for her to break the tense silence.

"Six of your students had to go home because of how scared they were." More than just a statement, it was a condemnation.

Janet couldn't stand Merriwether's glare, so she looked at the floor.

"Six times I had to explain to parents that what scared their child was a teacher yelling at an empty jacket."

Merriwether paused, but Janet couldn't speak. She knew what she'd seen. Even now she could see in her mind the boy in the red jacket stepping out from the coat rack. She didn't know what was happening to her, but she was scared. Fidgeting, she waited for Merriwether to get to the point, to bring the axe down.

"Six times I had to apologize, not only for the inconvenience of disrupting their schedule, but for the possible long-term effects such an incident might have on them."

Principal Merriwether stood, glanced out the window, then turned back toward Janet. She stared, waiting for Janet to wilt, but this time she didn't look away.

"I still don't understand why my predecessor had such high praise for you. But because of that, I am going to give you one more chance. You'll take the next two weeks off, during which you will carefully consider if teaching is really what you want to do."

Janet said nothing, just wiped her eyes. She didn't have the benefit of tenure or union protection. Earlyside was a private school, and she had little recourse.

"If you feel that teaching is your true calling, then you will need to prove it to me by changing your habits to reflect a level of dedication and professionalism that I have yet to see. Is that clear?"

Janet nodded.

"At the end of your two-week absence, I expect you to call me on that Friday, at 3:00 p.m. sharp, so we can discuss your future."

Janet, feeling like she was losing her mind, struggled to control her emotions. She wrapped her fingers around the armrests and squeezed to hold it all in.

"Is that understood?"

Janet nodded again.

"Then you may pick up your things from your classroom on your way out."

Janet, stunned into silence, could only stand and exit Merriwether's office.

3.

JANET TOOK a deep breath before looking through the window in the door to her classroom. Everyone sat in their math groups, working on simple addition problems. *My kids…they're moving on without me.* She already felt like a stranger in this place. The substitute stood at the board, gesturing and smiling as she spoke. The sub noticed Janet, and her smile faltered as she came over to the door.

"Can I help you?" the sub said as she opened it.

The class whispered as Janet entered.

"Who said you could talk?" the sub said, her tone harsher than what Janet would use.

The class laughed nervously, many of them trying to hide it behind their hands.

The substitute looked ready to yell at Janet's class. Her kids.

"Just ring the bell," Janet whispered.

"Excuse me?" she said, confused.

"The bell on the desk. You can ring it and they'll be quiet."

"And who are you?"

"I'm Miss Martlee. I came to get my things. I'm sorry for the interruption."

Janet could feel the children stare as she went to the front of the room and hastily loaded her things into her backpack.

"When will you be back?" Ukiah said, her voice small.

"In two weeks, hopefully. I just need… I need some rest. You all be extra good until then and do exactly what your teacher says. Okay?"

"Yes, Miss Martlee," the class said in unison.

Janet shouldered her backpack and hurried out before she started to cry.

A pair of teachers stopped talking when Janet entered the teachers' lounge. They sipped their coffee and watched as she wheeled her bike out. They started talking again even before the door had closed behind her. From their tone, news of her little breakdown had already circulated through the school.

Janet walked her bike to the sidewalk. She glanced up and saw Principal Merriwether watching her from the second-floor window. She got on the bike and pedaled away.

At first, she didn't know where she was going to go. It was still the middle of the school day. Normally, she turned to Angela in her time of need, but she was still at Earlyside teaching her fourth graders. Janet didn't want to go home to an empty apartment, didn't want to walk past the home office and wonder if she'd reacted too harshly about the crib. As she pedaled harder, she realized where she would go, where she must go. It felt good to push the pace, to make her legs ache and push even faster. It made it easier to quiet her thoughts, to keep her focus on the task of simply moving.

1.

SINCE THERE was no bike rack, Janet locked her bike to a light post outside the Howard King Medical Offices. She took a deep breath, feeling nervous despite her resolve. The doors opened with a soft whoosh. A half-dozen patients sat in chairs, reading magazines or staring at their cell phones. An old man looked up, gave her a lingering once over before returning to a wrinkled copy of Sports Illustrated.

Janet went to the receptionist's window and waited. A woman with eyebrows tweezed to faint pencil slashes ignored her for nearly a minute as she talked on the phone. Janet shifted from foot to foot and sighed audibly. The woman glanced over with a cocked brow.

"Okay, Dennis, I have to go. Yes, we'll have dinner. And what else? That depends." She giggled, snapped a bubble with her bubblegum. "I gotta go. Bye-bye-bye!" She hung up and turned to Janet.

"I'd like to see my doctor," Janet said.

"Sorry about that. It's my anniversary."

"Congratulations."

"Three months. I'm crazy about that guy." She tapped a key on her keyboard, and her face turned serious, and certainly more professional. "Who's your doctor again?"

"Dr. Gossett. My usual appointment is on Fridays. But I need to see her sooner. Right now, if possible."

The scheduler let out a doubtful groan and checked the computer. "Looks like she's booked until four."

"Could I see her then?"

"What's your name again?"

"Janet Martlee."

"Let me see if she's available, then I'll let you know."

5.

JANET SAT on a brown leather couch. She stared at the framed diploma on the wall—DePaul University. She'd started seeing Dr. Gossett after things got serious with Brian. She didn't turn to therapy because she felt stressed by their relationship. It was the exact opposite, her feelings of contentment, that made her want to finally deal with her tumultuous childhood. She'd found someone she'd cared about deeply, and she didn't want to ruin it because of her old baggage. Hopefully, it hadn't come to that.

Dr. Elaine Gossett sat in a chair across from her, a legal pad in her lap. She was gray-haired and always looked at her through a wise squint. Gossett had brought a certain level of mental comfort to Janet, and she trusted her.

"How old do you think he was?"

"Twelve, maybe."

"About the age your son would be."

Janet hadn't considered this. The realization fell on her like a bucket of cold water dumped on her head. She stared at Dr. Gossett, but her therapist kept up eye contact long enough that Janet had to look away. "So, what..." she said in a small voice, "you think I saw a ghost?"

"Not in the traditional sense. But as a projection of the unresolved feelings you have about your son's death? Absolutely."

Janet considered this. "I don't believe in ghosts."

"Neither do I. But I do believe that our emotions and memories can play out in...unexpected ways." Dr. Gossett smiled, and damn her, it was the soothing smile Janet both loved and hated. It immediately set her mind at ease, no matter how stressed out she was feeling. "Were you telling the truth when you said you don't know how he died?"

"Yes, and also when I said I don't want to talk about it."

"But that's why this is happening. And it's being compounded by the new pregnancy. The more you repress these memories and emotions, the harder they have to fight back."

Janet swallowed hard. "You think it'll get worse?"

"It already has. Hallucinations and a blackout like you described could be the last steps before you suffer a complete break from reality."

Her words were like a slap across the face. A complete break from reality? "What can I do?"

Dr. Gossett leaned over, looked at her intently. "Find out what happened."

"Call my parents, you mean."

"It's important you speak to your parents, but you can't do this over the phone. Most communication is nonverbal."

"Should I go see them?"

"You've got two weeks off. Right?"

"Isn't there some other way?" Janet said, the words themselves heavy. "I haven't been back there in…so many years."

"'The treasure you seek is in the cave you fear to enter,'" Gossett said.

"Who's that? Confucius?" Janet said, recognizing the quote.

"No, it's Joseph Campbell."

"But what if they won't tell me? Or what if they don't know?"

"If you find out that you can't find out, at least it's an answer."

"And then I'll stop seeing things?"

"I can't guarantee that, of course." Dr. Gossett stood from her chair. "But based on my work with similar cases? Yes."

Janet sighed.

Dr. Gossett picked up a business card from her desk. She wrote something on the back and handed it to Janet. "Here's my direct line. If you go and you need help, call me."

"Are you sure?"

Dr. Gossett gave her a look. Her therapist knew about her trust issues. "Of course, Janet. Not everyone is out to hurt you."

CHAPTER 4

I.

KNEELING NEXT TO her bed, Janet reached under it and pulled out a plastic bin full of wrapping paper. A lock of hair fell over her eyes and she pushed it back behind her ear. After setting aside the bin, she reached under the bed for a second one.

After blowing dust bunnies off the lid, she opened it. She reached inside for the cardboard box and hesitated, feeling on the precarious edge of a tipping point in her life. While taking a deep breath, she grabbed the cardboard box, and ripped the tape off.

Well, I guess that's that. No turning back now.

She picked up a bundle of photos and thumbed through them.

Most showed her as a young girl on the grounds of the almond orchard where she grew up back in Oakport.

She put the photos back and dug through the box until she found a locked diary. It was a kid's diary, pink and satiny. She ran a finger along the spine, then went to the jewelry box on top of her dresser. Inside a drawer of tangled necklaces, she grabbed a small key she'd hidden long ago.

She sat on the bed, unlocked the diary and flipped through the pages. It was full of writing and drawings, mostly juvenile.

She stopped when she came across a photo. The picture was a bookmark left at the last entry. Just seventeen, she's holding a baby wearing a blue onesie.

Oh, Joey.

Her heart ached as she stared at the photo. She remembered the tight grip of his tiny fists as he'd hold onto her when she carried him. The smell of his hair upon waking. The soft cooing laughter he never had the chance to grow out of. Feeling short of breath, she slumped to her side on the bed.

After a moment, she picked up the diary and read.

2.

BRIAN PULLED up to the old Victorian, tired from a long day at the office. He was a founding partner at Wundr, a social media startup, and he was starting to wonder if a new platform could ever breakthrough in an already saturated market. Even if his company could never take on the titans—Facebook, Instagram, or Twitter—if they were able to make their platform somehow unique, somehow essential to certain key demographics, the titans would seek to buy them out. Which wouldn't be the worst-case scenario. He could easily retire from the buyout of that business "failure."

His head was pounding with a budding migraine, and he didn't know what to expect when he went inside and saw Janet.

He loved her like no other person in his life. And he wanted to share that love, to marry her, have a baby with her.

He pulled the keys from the ignition and went to the front door.

Janet's past was complicated, and she rarely spoke about it. But…wasn't she supposed to share her life with him?

All he could do, he realized, was be supportive. He wanted her in his life, and she wanted him in hers.

We're meant to be together, he thought, like a mantra, but didn't know if he believed it.

When he walked inside, he saw Janet's bike leaning against the wall in the front hallway.

That's a good sign.

"Janet?" he called out. The apartment felt empty. The sun was setting and the rooms were dark. He flipped on a light switch. "Honey?"

He peeked inside the darkened kitchen. Empty.

As he made his way over to their bedroom, he fully expected it to be empty as well, perhaps her drawers thrown open and cleaned out. Instead, he found her asleep on the bed. A gaudy pink book was opened on her chest. He felt an intense relief that she was still here, and that she was safe.

He approached, his smile turning into a frown. Next to the opened book, she was holding a picture from when she was younger. In the photo, she was holding a baby on her lap.

He slipped it from her grasp and sat on the bed next to her. Janet stirred awake. She smiled warmly when she saw him, then noticed he was holding the picture.

"Is this what I don't understand?" Brian said. "Did you have another baby?"

"I was a kid. Seventeen. He died," she said bluntly. She looked away, blinked to stave off tears.

"What? Really?" Brian's anger disappeared by this revelation. He touched her leg. She flinched and he pulled back his hand. He wanted to take her into his arms, but he could tell she didn't want the physical contact. "How?"

"I don't know."

"What do you mean? How can you not know?"

"Because I didn't want to know."

Her forcefulness startled him.

"The whole thing was a mess," she said, sitting up higher on her pillow. "Like I said, I was seventeen. Ethan, the boy who got me pregnant, was my next-door neighbor. He was nineteen. My dad flipped out. Pressed charges for statutory rape. Got him sent to jail for a few months. My dad hated me after that. Wouldn't even look at me."

Janet took the picture from Brian, stared at it. He expected her to look at it with longing, but instead, he saw confusion.

"Then one day I woke up in the hospital. They said I'd been in a coma for three days and Joey was dead. I ran away later on that night. Angela had graduated two years before and was here for college. She let me live with her. Helped me with everything. Getting my GED. My teaching credentials. Even the job at Earlyside."

"Jesus..." Brian said. "I never would have gotten you that crib if I'd known about this."

"I know. Now it's my turn to say sorry. I should have told you."

"It's okay. It all makes sense now. Especially why you didn't want to talk about it."

"Good. Because there's something I need to do."

"Name it." He meant what he'd said. Whatever she needed, he'd be there for her.

"Dr. Gossett wants me to go home. To find out what happened."

Brian rubbed his hands together, ready to tackle this head-on. "Great. When do we leave?"

"I'm going alone."

"Janet, please. Let me help you."

"You can. By letting me do this the way I need to."

He paused. His throat tightened with emotion. "Okay."

Janet hugged him tightly, but he was still not pleased.

3.

JANET SAT across from Angela at a table next to the window of their favorite coffee shop, empty cups and crumb-filled plates in front of them.

"Well, this sucks."

"I'm sorry," Angela shrugged, "but I can't say it's a good idea when I don't think it is."

"Dr. Gossett's a professional," Janet said.

"And that makes her the Pope? This just sounds crazy. Like, it'll cause more harm than good."

"I need to know."

"So find out about Joey some other way. Call the police. The hospital. Anyone but your parents."

"She said I have to face everything I ran away from."

"Including Ethan?"

"I doubt he's still around." While her thoughts had been focused on Joey, it was impossible to think of her son without also thinking about his dad.

"Okay. I tried. But don't blame me when this makes things worse."

"Is that really what you think will happen?"

"I hope not. I really do. But I remember your dad. I don't want you to get hurt like that again. Promise me you'll leave at the first sign of trouble."

Janet took a deep breath, then nodded.

"Are you sure I can't come with you?" Angela stuck out her bottom lip and batted her eyes.

Janet cracked a smile. "You've always been there for me, and I love you for it. But I need to do this on my own. It's time."

4.

THE MORNING was cool and fog hung low in the hills surrounding the bay. Standing next to Brian's car, Janet felt a shiver.

Brian lifted a second suitcase and set it into the open trunk. "Don't you think you should at least let them know you're coming?"

"I don't want to give myself the chance to back out. And by doing this on my own terms, I'm in control. Understand?"

"Not really. But what else is new?"

He handed her the keys, and his fingers lingered on hers.

"Babe..."

"I love you," he said, filling the silence.

"Thank you. For everything. I love you, too. So much."

"Call me as soon as you get there. And if you change your mind and want me to join you, I will."

"I'm sure that won't be necessary."

"Stop using that as the only reason for anything. Art isn't necessary. People still do it."

"That's where you're wrong. Art is necessary. That's why people do it. It's obviously not for the money."

"I just got womansplained." He laughed softly.

"Yeah, you did."

She kissed him on the lips. He hesitated, for a moment, then fully returned the pressure, the longing already building between them.

He broke away, cocked an eyebrow. "You better go before I change my mind about letting you use my car."

"You sure you'll be okay?"

"Yes. Go!"

Janet hopped in the Mazda and started the engine. As she backed out of the drive, he watched her go, his hands in his pockets, slowly swaying forward and back. He smiled, but it was a sad smile. He looked like a lost little boy. She hoped she hadn't damaged their relationship beyond the point of repair.

As she pulled away, she looked over and gave a little wave. But Brian had already turned toward the door, his head low.

Janet passed over the Golden Gate Bridge as the fog began to dissipate. Before long, she was driving north through the Robin Williams Tunnel, through scenic hills she never grew tired of seeing. It helped the miles tick away, and soon, the houseboats in Sausalito were bobbing in the water off to her right. She passed Vallejo, the familiar Jelly Belly factory; she cut a fine ribbon across Rio Vista, and as she crossed the Sacramento River, the flat delta gave way to farmland. Each scenic marker another moment pushing her past the point of no return. Her anxiety ratcheted with each mile eclipsed, and she saw familiar touchstones in the landscape she didn't even realize she still remembered.

After an hour through the winding farm fields, the fine blacktop became a cracked road lined on both sides with almond orchards like the one in the photos from the bin under her bed. She made one final turn, and where she'd expected to see a gnarled oak tree at the corner of the driveway, there was only a bare stump cut to knee-height. A flower pot full of rust-colored mums sat atop the stump of the tree she used to climb as a child.

She checked the oversized black mailbox on its rusted metal post at the other side of the driveway. The hand-painted letters were faded, but she could still make out the name "MARTLEE."

Janet stared ahead, drummed her fingers on the steering wheel. She felt something weighty inside herself, and her eyes were shiny with the threat of tears.

Before she could totally lose it, she opened her wallet and fished out the business card Dr. Gossett had given her before she left. She turned it over, read what she'd written on the back: The treasure you seek is in the cave you fear to enter.

Janet took a steadying breath, put the card away, and took her foot off the brake. The car idled ahead, and soon a sprawling, three-story yellow Victorian with a large veranda, dormer windows, and gabled roof became fully visible as she pulled past the trees in the front yard.

In Janet's childhood photos, it was beautiful. Not anymore.

The filigree was broken. The porch sagged at a dangerous angle.

Most of the windows were covered with warped plywood. And the doors had two-by-fours nailed across them like bars.

Janet stared blankly. She hadn't expected anything like this. She opened her purse and found a piece of paper with a number written on it. She removed her cell phone from the holder on the dash and dialed as she got out of the car.

She leaned against the car. When the call connected, she heard the phone ringing inside the house.

Her eyes drifted up to a window in the turret on the third floor, not covered with a board.

Something—a shadow of some kind—was holding the white lace curtain aside. The curtain dropped. She immediately thought of the boy in the red jacket.

Janet froze. The phone kept ringing.

A few seconds later, a boy did indeed come running out from the back of the house. "Hey!" she shouted.

This was certainly not a ghost. He was lively and obviously scared that she'd discovered him. Not only that, but his skin was not the sickly blue-white like the boy in the red jacket. This kid had darker skin. He might've been Hispanic, but she didn't get a good look at him.

He didn't stop, didn't even glance back in her direction. Before Janet could decide to chase him, he ran out of sight behind the barn.

What the heck is going on?

Janet noticed the phone still ringing. She ended the call and pocketed her phone, then went around to the back of the house.

The door into the mud room was open. A pile of two-by-fours leaned against the wall next to it, as if they'd been pried away. Janet entered the darkened interior cautiously.

She paused to let her eyes adjust to the dim light as she passed through. The air felt heavy, enclosed, stale. As if no one had lived here in a long time. Yet, even with that, the smell of her childhood home was familiar.

She stepped into the living room, bars of yellow light beaming through the gaps in the boards covering the front windows. The furniture was all still there, but now covered in dusty white sheets. She glanced toward the stairs as she returned to the kitchen.

Right when she was trying to figure out why dishes were drying in the rack by the sink, the refrigerator cycled loudly, startling her. She went over and opened it. Fresh food was inside. She picked up the jug of milk, then chanced smelling it. Not even sour.

How very weird.

She returned it to the fridge, then went through the mudroom and out the back door.

Janet walked backward for a handful of steps, taking in the details of her old house, trying to discover what might've happened here in her absence. She climbed into the car, rolled down the window, and gave the house one last long look before driving away.

CHAPTER 5

I.

DOWNTOWN OAKPORT WAS packed with post-Gold Rush architecture but was too rundown to attract antique seekers from the city. There had been peaks and valleys in the ensuing one hundred and seventy years, but the latest lull had dragged on for decades without any sign of improving.

Most of the storefronts were vacant and boarded-up. The few that weren't were decidedly low-end: selling second-hand clothing, used books, a pawn shop, the local food pantry.

Janet drove to the police station at the end of Main Street and had no trouble finding a parking spot out front. When she entered the station, a bell jangled over the door.

She'd almost forgotten his name, but as soon as Chief Harold Keegin came out from his office, the name popped into her head. He spat into the empty soda can he was carrying, then wiped his bushy mustache with the back of his hand as he stepped up behind the long counter.

He paused, gaping at her, then his eyes widened. "I'll be damned. Janet Martlee, in the flesh. I thought I was seeing a ghost."

"You've got quite a memory, Chief Keegin." The chief had been on the job long enough that he was in charge during Ethan's arrest, and later on, Joey's death.

"My wife would disagree. Your mother didn't tell me that she'd found you."

"She didn't."

"Then who did?"

"Nobody."

"You're not here because of your dad's accident?"

"What? No. I didn't know he'd been in one."

"Had a stroke. Fell off a ladder. Maybe the other way around. He's in a hospital in Sacramento."

Her thoughts were so conflicted. "Will he be okay?"

"Don't know yet. Your mother says his right side is paralyzed and he can't talk. So what brings you all the way back here, then?"

"I went to the house."

"Your folks haven't lived there for going on two years."

"Well, somebody is."

"Come again?" Keegin blinked rapidly.

"There was a boy inside. He ran away when he saw me. Plus, there's fresh food in the refrigerator."

Keegin furrowed his brow and headed to a radio.

"That's Gabriel, probably," he said, and picked up the microphone. "He's Facundo Mardinez's son. Facundo is the guy your dad hired to keep the orchard going. But Gabriel's not supposed to be in the house."

Keegin spat into the soda can again.

"Excuse me." He clicked the button on the microphone a few times, as if out of habit, then kept it pressed as he brought it to his lips. "Skovil, what's your 20?"

The radio crackled and hissed, then the channel cleared, and Skovil replied. "I'm 10-64 at Dainty's."

"Put the corn dog down and get over to the Martlee place."

Janet turned away and noticed the bulletin board on the wall, crammed with missing persons flyers.

"Why?" Skovil said.

"The Mardinez kid is going in the house again." Keegin sighed in exasperation. "Tell him to stop it."

"10-4," Skovil replied.

Keegin set the microphone down. Janet turned to face him.

"Sorry about that," he said, his cheeks flushed with anger.

"So, my parents are still in town?"

"More or less. They moved to a smaller place. It was getting to be a pain for them to keep up the old house. See here?" He pointed at a spot on a map under the glass countertop. "That's Delta Palms. Trailer park up the road toward Locke. By the marina. Number...yeah, I believe, it's 23."

Janet typed the info into her phone.

"You should be prepared," Keegin said.

"For what?"

"No soft way to put it," Keegin said, looking like he didn't want to finish the thought. "I'm not sure your mother'll be glad you're here."

"I'm not sure I am, either."

"Fair enough. But if that's the case, why'd you come back? After all this time, I mean."

"I'm spelunking," she said and slipped her phone into her pocket.

He wrinkled his brow, not really understanding. "One more thing. Ethan Frewel owns Dainty's now. So do everyone a favor and eat somewhere else."

Keegin spit into his can, and that was enough of a punctuation mark to end their conversation.

2.

WHEN JANET started to back out of her parking spot in front of the police station, she had to slam on the brakes when an Oakport police car passed by in a rush.

The officer behind the wheel steered with one hand, while he held a half-eaten corndog in the other. Janet smiled. But it all but vanished when she saw movement in the station windows. When she looked up, Chief Keegin—with his phone to his ear—watched her through his office window.

He backed away from the blinds as Janet pulled into traffic, but not before she double-checked to make sure the road was clear.

The way to Delta Palms and her parents' trailer was on the other side of town, but she didn't head in that direction right away. Instead, she took her time looking at the depressing storefronts, remembering happier times.

She knew she would drive past Dainty's, even if she had trouble admitting it to herself. Why else was she lingering downtown?

Dainty's appeared at the edge of town, a 1950s style diner with a neon sign in the window that proclaimed "World's Best Corn Dog!"

As Janet passed, she slowed enough to catch a glimpse of Ethan Frewel serving a plate to a customer. As he set the plate stacked high with pancakes on the table, his smile alone was reason enough for her heart to skip a beat. She had fallen for Ethan long before he knew her name. And then, once he had noticed her, he became her entire life from the time she was fifteen until she left town three years later.

She faced forward, her brow knitted with worry, and accelerated over the edge of town and into the surrounding woods.

The road, built on top of the levee, followed the curves of the Sacramento River. Janet cruised along carefully. In quiet Oakport, you never knew when you'd come across a deer in the road, or a couple on a late-night walk.

Eventually, after getting turned around more than once on streets she used to know like the back of her hand, Janet drove across a bridge, under an arch that read "Delta Palms Trailer Park."

She'd known about the Palms when she was a kid, but she'd never actually been inside. Driving up and down the rows of tired tin boxes sardined together along the riverfront, she couldn't seem to locate number 23. She pulled to the side of the road next to the trailer park's playground. A half-dozen pre-teens chased each other around the monkey bars. It was refreshing seeing kids outside, having fun and burning off some energy.

Her smile faded when she noticed a boy in a dark red jacket standing under the slide, his back to her. Her heart started to race. She was reaching for the door handle, ready to run out and confront him, when he stepped out of the shadows, yelling, "Ready or not, here I come!"

Jesus, Janet. Get things under control. It was only the shadows under the slide playing tricks on you.

The rest of the children laughed and ran as the boy chased them. Janet shook her head, which was starting to pulse with the beginnings of a tension headache, and drove away.

After another ten minutes of methodically checking every address number, Janet found number 23. She pulled into the spare parking spot in the gravel drive. She stared at the windows, wondering about her sanity, and Dr. Gossett's as well, as she waited for…something.

Eventually, she exited the car and headed for the door. When she lifted her hand to knock, the door opened, and she stood staring face-to-face with her mother, with just the screen door between them. Her mom was shorter than she remembered, thirty pounds overweight, and topped with an old lady crewcut that said she didn't care what you thought.

"I hope you didn't come here looking for forgiveness." Her mom crossed her arms.

"No. I'm on doctor's orders."

"What kind?"

Janet blinked. "What do you mean?"

"Your doctor. What kind is he? Like Dr. Phil or Dr. Oz?"

"It's a she. And she's more of a Dr. Phil."

"Oh, I see. It's to be a scene, then, is it?"

"I hope not."

"That makes two of us."

They stared at one another for another few seconds. Neither budged. Neither emoted. Finally, her mom unlocked the screen door and pushed it open.

"Come on then."

Janet cautiously stepped inside.

Her mom noticed her judging the mess: newspapers, laundry, knitting, and dirty dishes.

"I know. I didn't realize it was this bad until Harry Keegin called and told me you were on your way over."

"Understandable," Janet said. "Especially with Dad in the hospital."

"What else did he tell you?"

"He didn't think you'd be glad to see me. And I should stay away from Dainty's."

Her mom started to say something, but the phone rang and she rushed to look at the caller ID. "It's the hospital." She picked up the receiver. "Martlee residence. Doris speaking."

Doris listened for a moment, then closed her eyes. The tears came out anyway.

Janet stepped closer. She could hear the tone of the voice on the other end of the line, but not the meaning of the words.

"Okay…okay, I'll be there as soon as I can." She hung up, her hand lingered on the set, her eyes cast low.

Janet braced for the worst. "Mom, what is it?"

"He's…gone into a coma now."

Janet held her arms open. After a slight hesitation, her mom stepped into them. The barrier between them was down. For the moment, anyway.

"Will you go with me?" Her mom's voice was frail, and for the first time, sounded old.

"I'll drive."

3.

AS THEY headed toward the city, the flat farmland was overtaken by cookie-cutter suburban subdivisions.

"What does he do for work?"

"He's a social media engineer."

"Whatever that is," her mom said, pursing her lips as if she'd tasted something sour. "Are you sure you're not making that up?"

"Absolutely. He works at a startup. It's early still, but promising."

"How long have you been together?"

"A little over a year."

Her mom glanced at her. "You're not wearing a ring."

"Not yet."

"Planning on it, then?"

"I'm pregnant," Janet said, and the air inside the car became leaden. Neither spoke right away. The suburban homes blurred by the windows.

"Oh, I see," her mom said and let out a long sigh. "So that's what this is all about. Your doctor wanted you to give us a second chance at being grandparents. Is that it?"

"Not exactly," she said. "I mean, that's part of it, I guess. But the main reason I'm here is to find out what happened with Joey."

"What do you mean 'find out?' You know what happened."

"Actually...I don't remember. There's a big gaping black hole in my memory around that time."

"What about the car crash?"

"The what?" Janet looked away from the road, half expecting her mom to be grinning as if pulling her leg. She was definitely not.

"You really don't remember?"

Janet looked back at the road, not liking her mom's tone. "Do you think I'd be here otherwise?"

"You took your father's car in the middle of the night. And in your pajamas! Didn't get more than a mile from the house before you hit a tree and went into the river."

"And Joey, was he with me? Is that what happened to him?"

"No. You found him first. Then you drove away because you were so upset."

"Where was he? Where did I find him?"

"In his crib. Dr. Lawter said it was SIDS. You really don't remember any of this?"

Janet shook her head, bit her lower lip.

Doris sighed again. "I know your note told us not to try to find you, but you could've at least called to say you were okay."

"I know. I'm sorry."

"I thought you weren't looking for forgiveness."

"I didn't think I was."

She drove on, and they passed the rest of the time to the hospital in silence.

4.

"I WANT you to brace yourself," her mom said, pausing outside hospital room 301. "He doesn't look well. Not at all."

Janet nodded and followed her into the room.

Her dad was reclined in a gatch bed, propped up with pillows, hooked to a telemetry transmitter and an IV. He really did look unwell. A shell of the man from her memories. Even when they'd fought when Janet was a teen, Wayne Martlee had always been hale and hearty.

A nurse glanced at them as she finished adjusting his nasal cannula, then headed for the door. "I'm just wrapping up. I'll tell Dr. Prevesh you're here, Mrs. Martlee."

"Thanks, Maggie," her mom said softly.

Janet stared at the cast on her dad's right arm and the scabbed-over scratches on his face. "How far did he fall?"

"I don't know. I didn't see it happen. We were working at the house. But I was inside."

A doctor entered the room. He had a well-trimmed beard. A stethoscope hung around his neck.

"Hello, Mrs. Martlee." He reached out and shook her hand.

"Dr. Prevesh."

He turned to Janet and held out his hand to her. "And who are you?"

"This is my daughter, Janet."

Janet shook his hand, which was soft and warm.

"Nice to meet you, Janet. I'm glad to see your mother is getting the help she needs."

"Someone," her mom said, hooking a thumb at the doctor, "thinks I need help."

"You do! But like so many of your generation, you confuse asking for help with weakness." Dr. Prevesh turned to Janet again. "Please tell me you'll be staying with her for a few days."

"We hadn't talked about it yet, but I think so. I hope so," Janet said, and she only now realized she really meant it. Maybe Dr. Gossett had been on to something.

"Very good."

Janet's phone buzzed. As she took it out, Dr. Prevesh waved his finger at her.

"Sorry, Miss Martlee. You can't use that in here."

Janet read a text from Brian: Are U there yet? She gave her mom an apologetic look. "It's Brian. I just need to let him know what's happening."

"You can use it in the waiting area near the elevators," the doctor said.

"Thanks."

Janet headed for the door. She glanced back, saw her mom looking down at her dad. He was emaciated, his skin a grayish hue. Her mother had always been so strong, but with all this, she could see cracks forming in her formidable exterior.

As she neared the elevators, she dialed her phone. As it connected, she looked out the window, saw an old man wearing a robe over his hospital gown, walking and smoking a cigarette.

Brian's line picked up. "You okay?" he said, cutting through any preamble.

"Yeah," she said, surprised how choked up she felt. "Well, I'm fine. I'm here. I tracked down Mom. It's a long story, but they're living in a depressing trailer park called Delta Palms."

"Is that where you're at?"

"No, I'm at the hospital."

"Jesus, are you okay?"

"Yeah. I'm fine. Mom's fine…" She paused, collecting herself. "Dad was working on the house. They're trying to fix it up to sell. He fell off the roof and broke some bones, suffered a stroke. He just slipped into a coma."

"My God, that's awful."

"I know. I ducked out of his room to call you, so I can't talk long."

"Of course. Did you tell her why you're there yet?"

"I did. She said Joey died of SIDS and I was in the hospital because I crashed my dad's car."

"Well, that's good. That you got an answer, I mean. Isn't it?"

Janet watched the old man blow smoke rings.

"Janet? Are you still there?"

The old man snubbed out his cigarette and walked back inside, a cloud of cigarette smoke hovering over him as if it were permanently attached to him.

"I don't think that's what happened," Janet said finally.

"I thought you couldn't remember?"

"I didn't have a scratch, Brian. I remember that much. My dad fell off a ladder, and he's got a broken arm and his face is all cut up. But after the car crash…nothing. I had a headache, that's about it."

"Why would she lie to you?"

"I don't know. But there must be a reason. And that's what I have to find out. Obviously."

"Ask the hospital. They'd have the records, wouldn't they?"

Janet looked up to see Dr. Prevesh exiting her dad's room.

"Good idea. I'll call you later."

"Okay. Just…be careful. Promise?"

"Sure. I have to go."

"Bye."

She hung up without replying, then hurried to catch up with the doctor.

"Excuse me, Doctor."

Dr. Prevesh stopped and turned around.

"Can I get copies of records from when I was a patient here?"

"That depends." He tilted his head, considering. "How long ago?"

"Twelve years."

"Out of luck, I'm afraid. We're only required to keep seven years."

"Would my doctor have them?"

"Maybe. Who was it?"

"Dr. Lawter."

"William Lawter?"

There was something strange in the doctor's voice. "I think so," Janet said. "Is something wrong?"

"I'm surprised you don't know. It was national news. He poisoned six of his patients."

"On purpose?"

"Yes. He believed they were involved in human sacrifice or something. He was insane, of course."

Doris came out of the room behind them. "Who was insane?"

"Dr. Lawter," Janet said.

"I'll say. I knew all the victims, you know. Not well. But well enough to say hello if we saw each other at the grocery store."

"Is he still alive?"

"Last I heard, he was. At the state psychiatric hospital in Napa." He glanced at his watch. "Is there anything else?"

Janet shook her head.

"I'm glad you're here, Janet. Make sure your mom is eating and getting plenty of rest."

"I'll do my best. She's stubborn. The only person she really listens to is…" she hesitated, "is Dad."

Dr. Prevesh pursed his lips and nodded. He headed off toward the nurses' station.

"What were you asking about Dr. Lawter for?"

"My doctor wanted to see the file on my first pregnancy," Janet said, quickly inventing a reason other than the truth.

"What's a Dr. Phil doctor need to see that for?"

"No. My Dr. Oz doctor."

"Oh. That makes sense. Want me to take you to lunch?"

Janet smiled, but it never reached her eyes. "That would be nice."

5.

JANET AND Doris sat together at a table in the corner of the hospital cafeteria. Janet picked through a salad as limp as wet newspaper.

"I don't understand," Janet said. "If the Frewels want the property, why don't you just sell it to them?"

"You know your father. He can't let anything go. Ethan took his little girl's purity, after all." She tilted her head and grinned, knowing how ridiculous it sounded.

Janet frowned as she pushed her plate away. "But it's been twelve years."

"I know. And I just about had him convinced it was okay. That's why we were at the house. Fixing things. Then he had the stroke and had his fall. And now this."

"I can help while I'm here."

"Help with what?"

"Fixing the house. Whatever it was you were doing."

"What do you know about any of that?"

"Nothing. But Google does."

"Who's Google?"

"Please tell me you're joking."

"About what?"

Janet shook her head and closed her eyes.

6.

LATER ON, after spending another hour or so with her dad, they left the hospital. Janet drove with her mom in the passenger seat. Her mom held Janet's cell phone, and she was staring at it intently as she spoke into the Google app.

"What. Year. Was. Elvis. Presley. Born?"

The phone replied right away. "Elvis Presley was born on January 8th, 1935."

"It's like Star Trek."

"Why don't you ask something we need to know?"

"Like what?"

"How to take boards off windows."

"How about," her mom said, "Why. Is. My. Daughter. Such. A. Wise. Ass?"

7.

"I THINK this is a bad idea," her mom said as she watched Janet pull the rope on an extension ladder to place it between two boarded-up windows on the second floor.

"No. The bad idea was Dad thinking he could do it by himself."

"You know your father."

"Yeah, but haven't you heard that people over sixty shouldn't go climbing on ladders?"

Apparently, her mom didn't have a snide reply because she just shrugged.

"Give me the hammer and hold the ladder like I showed you."

Her mom handed Janet the hammer, then gripped the ladder tightly. "Please be careful."

"You worry too much." Janet climbed up, only feeling a slight swirl of vertigo as she neared the top. Once in position, she wedged the claw-end of the hammer under the plywood board and pried it up. She then pushed the wood back down and started pulling the exposed nail heads.

"See that?" Janet said, looking down. "Just like the video."

Her mom frowned, obviously still scared, as Janet worked her way along the bottom edge first. Then she lifted the top right corner and pushed the board back down.

When she pulled that nail, the board swung to the left, revealing a face behind the glass.

"What the hell?" Janet gasped, nearly losing her balance, but then she realized it was only a mannequin.

"What happened?"

"That stupid mannequin in your sewing room. I hate that thing."

Her mom guffawed. "Remember how your father used to scare you with it at Halloween?"

"Why do you think I hate it?"

Janet hung the hammer on a rung, then pulled the board off the wall and carefully climbed down.

At the bottom, she dropped the board flat and dusted her hands. "See. Nothing to it. We'll be done before dark, easy. With plenty of time to stop at the hardware store. We need some wood putty to seal the nail holes."

"And the pharmacy, don't forget."

Janet hadn't seen her mom in so long. They were practically strangers, yet, here she was helping out, somehow managing to bridge the gap between them. She was starting to wonder if she'd wasted all those estranged years for no reason.

CHAPTER 6

I.

JANET STARED AT all the smiling faces on the missing persons flyers.

One flyer stood among the many. The picture for a twelve-year-old named Ricky Wozner was partly covered. She had to lift the one on top to fully see it. When she did, her eyes widened. He looked exactly like the boy in the dark red jacket.

Officer Skovil came in noisily through a door at the back of the station.

"See someone you know?" Skovil said.

She jerked as if she'd been caught doing something unseemly. "No. I'm just surprised there are so many...I mean, for a small town like this."

"None of them are from here. Other agencies send them because Oakport is on the way to a lot of places."

Skovil set a folder on the glass-topped counter and opened it, then took out a sheet of paper and handed it to her. "Here's the report on Joseph. SIDS. Like you said."

He handed her a second sheet of paper.

"Uh...thanks."

"Copy of the death certificate, signed by Dr. Lawter."

It was harder for Janet to look at this one.

"And here's the report on the car accident."

Janet took the third piece of paper and looked at it closely. "Not much to it, is there?"

"There shouldn't be, really. Neither one of these things was a crime. Your baby died of natural causes." He paused long enough she looked up from the papers. "And no other car was involved in your accident."

As Janet scanned the pages again, she felt disappointed that the details matched what Doris told her.

"You okay?" He scratched the stubble on his chin. "It's a lot to take in."

"Yes. You've been very helpful."

"Doesn't seem like it."

"I'm sorry. You have, really. It's just difficult. Digging this up. Thank you again."

"Anytime. And if you need anything else while you're in town, give me a holler and I'll do what I can."

2.

LATER ON, Janet opened the door for her mom as they exited Oakport Drugs.

"So, you will?" Janet asked. "Will you take me there?"

Her mom curled over the lip of the prescription bag. "Of course. After all, you never did get to see the marker I picked."

Janet didn't understand.

"You ran away before the funeral. Remember?"

This hit Janet hard. She tried valiantly not to show it, but her mom obviously noticed.

"Are you sure this is a good idea?" her mom said.

"No. It's not. But that's why I need to do it." Though her words had strength behind them, on the inside she felt uncertain. Stopping in her tracks, she tried to recall the quote Dr. Gossett had told her during her last session, the words that had felt so reassuring at the time.

"What you need to do?" Her mom stopped and looked back over her shoulder. "Whatever the heck that means."

"Do you know who Joseph Campbell is?" The quote came back to her in a flash, fully-formed: The treasure you seek is in the cave you fear to enter.

"Isn't he a baseball player?"

Janet groaned. "Never mind. Come on. Let's get going."

They reached the car, and when her mom was ready to delve further into what she was talking about, Janet started the engine and turned on the radio. A jangly pop song filled the silence as she pulled away.

3.

ST. PETER'S Church was a rough-hewn Gothic building with a steep slate roof and narrow bell tower. A large cemetery spread out behind it, surrounded by a gray stone wall topped with black wrought-iron spikes.

Janet went up to the gate leading to the cemetery, and tried to open it, but it was locked.

"What now?" Janet said.

"Let's try the rectory."

They walked along the stone wall. The doorway to the rectory was tucked in the corner of the property with the church and graveyard beyond. Another low gate blocked the path.

"Here, let's try this." Her mom pointed to an intercom. She pressed the button.

The speaker gave off a low hiss, then someone said, "Hello, how may I help you?"

"Father Rozaro?"

"Yes."

"It's Doris Martlee. I'm here with my daughter. Can we speak to you? It's about what I mentioned on the phone."

"Certainly, my child. I will be right out." The speaker clicked off.

Father Rozaro opened the rectory's heavy oaken door and stepped outside. He wore black pants and a black shirt with a tabbed collar. His gray hair was close-cropped and neat, while he sported an unruly mustache.

"Hello, Father," her mother said.

"So good to see you, Doris. How is Wayne?"

"He's fighting."

"I'm praying for him."

"I know, Father. Thank you."

The priest unlocked the gate and waved them through. They walked along a cobbled walkway between the rectory that led to the front of the church. When they reached the door, the priest held it open to let the women inside as they entered the narthex.

"I'm sorry about the locked gate," Father Rozaro said in a hushed tone. "We can cut through the church to access the cemetery."

"That's new. Did something happen?" her mom said.

"Vandals, that's what happened! I used to be able to keep the church open all the time. Not anymore!" He walked to a blinking keypad and punched in a code for the alarm system. "Now it has to be locked and alarmed and monitored with cameras."

"The angels didn't stop them?" Janet said, unable to keep the snark from her tone.

Her mom scowled at her.

Father Rozaro smiled. "I am quite certain the angels are waiting until those responsible arrive in purgatory before they deliver the appropriate punishment." Then he pulled open the nave door and gestured for them to follow. "After you, ladies."

Doris gave Janet another scowl for good measure.

The only light inside the nave came through the stained-glass windows. In spite of herself, Janet was awestruck for a moment. The light dazzled in myriad colors, and as they walked, the saintly figures seemed to move.

She fell behind and had to hurry to catch up with Father Rozaro and her mom as they went through a side door in the transept.

When she caught up to them, Father Rozaro and her mom were in the graveyard, walking among the headstones. Many were old and faded, with dates going back to the 1870s. She slowed, out of respect, and by the time she reached them, her mom glared at her over her shoulder.

They passed several large above-ground mausoleums, family names carved in stone banners over their gated entrances. They reached a raised patch of grass, surrounded by a foot-high wrought-iron fence.

Inside was a checkerboard pattern of child-sized crypt lids, each with its own marker. Her mom pointed at one made of dark blue marble that read: "JOSEPH P. MARTLEE. An Angel Here. An Angel Now, Forever."

Janet noticed a wilted sunflower laid between the marker and the crypt lid. She reached out to touch it, but pulled up short. "Where'd that come from?"

Her mom and Father Rozaro traded uncomfortable glances.

"Ethan," Rozaro said. "I see him at mass once or twice a year." Father Rozaro pointed to the far side of the cemetery. "His family plot is over there."

Janet glanced back, but only to avoid confronting how ill-prepared she was for this.

My boy...my Joey...I'm so sorry... After a beat, she faced Joey's grave again.

Overcome with emotion, she covered her mouth with one hand, then crouched and leaned forward on her knees.

"Would you like us to give you a moment?" the priest asked.

"No. Stay. Please."

Janet reached her hand up without looking. Her mom took it, squeezed.

"Joey, my baby," Janet whispered. "I'm so, so sorry."

She fought back tears, but it was a losing battle. Fat drops hit the marble and ran along the carved letters. Father Rozaro put his hand on her shoulder.

Janet kissed her fingers, then touched the marker carefully, as if it might be hot.

4.

JANET'S FACE was blank as she pulled away from the church. She could feel her mom staring at her with concern from the passenger's seat.

"You sure you're going to be okay?" her mom said.

"Yes, I'm sure. Quit asking."

As they drove past Dainty's Diner, Janet slowed to glance through the windows again. Instead of Ethan, she saw a waitress carrying a heavy tray to a table, her smile forced and barely there.

"He was married for a while," her mom said.

"Who? Father Rozaro?"

Her mom gave her a look. Caught, Janet sighed, as Dainty's disappeared from the rearview mirror.

"Did they have kids?" Janet said.

"Two boys. She took them when they got divorced. Moved to Florida, or somewhere. Said she wanted to make sure he never saw them again."

"How do you know all this?"

"When people blame you for things, they let you know."

5.

JANET SAT at the table, watching her mom at the stove, serving up scrambled eggs, hash browns, and sausage.

"I don't know how long it's been since I had breakfast for dinner."

"Dad never wanted to, remember?" her mom said. "But I like it, and it's easy."

"What did he used to say? Oh yeah, 'Backwards Ain't Right,' " she said, deepening her voice.

"He still says that about a lot of things."

"I'm sure. Especially these days. Please tell me he didn't vote for—"

"Of course, he did! But then I mistook the trash can for the mailbox when I went to send in his mail-in ballot."

"You didn't. Did you?"

"Not that it matters either way, but I am sleeping better these days about my decision."

Her mom started laughing, and it was infectious, as always. Soon, Janet laughed right along with her.

6.

IT WAS full-on night when Janet carried a shovel from the barn toward the house. When she heard a baby cry, she stopped and looked up. The third-floor window was open, the white curtains blowing in the breeze like shimmering spiderwebs.

When the baby cried again, she realized it was behind her.

She faced the orchard and stared at the lines of trees, searching for movement.

The baby cried more frantically. Janet hurried forward, the sound getting louder, charging through the first row of the orchard trees. She paused, listening. Her heart was pounding so hard, it thrummed in her ears and dampened her hearing. She moved cautiously into the next row and stopped in front of a tree, one that was different from the others.

The tree's bark was white, its blossoms as black as beetle backs. She reached out to touch a flower petal. When the baby cried again, Janet flinched, fearing the tree was making the sound.

But then she heard a cracking sound, like two great stones hitting each other, and then a hand—too big to be a baby's—broke through the ground at the base of the trunk.

Janet gasped and dropped to her knees. She clawed at the dirt, but it was too tough. Luckily, she had the shovel. She stepped back a pace, measured up the shovel's blade, and stomped on the back of it.

Blood, thick and glistening red, welled up around the blade. Janet yanked the shovel out and turned the dirt over with her hands. The clumps of dirt were saturated in sticky wetness.

She dug faster, maniacally, and soon a shape took form inside the widening hole. She dropped the shovel, went to her hands and knees, and brushed away the dirt. Yes, it was an arm. An arm wearing a dark red jacket. More dirt fell away, exposing a pallid neck grimed with dirty streaks of blood. She pulled on the arm, as if urging the boy to stand.

Because it was the boy from her classroom. The little boy with his red jacket and familiar eyes. She brushed the dirt from his face. Such a sweet boy!

She kept working, exposing more of him.

Soil dusted his eye lashes and as she wiped her palm against his face. His ghastly eyes opened, and the skin of his blue face began to tense, as if in anger, and his muscles twitched, and when he opened his mouth to speak, the grating of his vocal cords was such a horrible, wounded sound.

Janet stumbled backward, screaming—

7.

SHE AWOKE with a start on the couch, gasping for breath.

For a moment, she was confused about where she was. But then she saw the smiling photo of her parents—one taken after she'd moved away—looking down at her from the wall across from her. She grabbed her laptop from the end table. When the screen lit up, she checked the time: 3:13 a.m.

She pulled up Google and typed "Ricky Wozner" into the search bar.

The first link in the search revealed a news story. She whispered the headline, "Fairvale Boy Still Missing One Year After Disappearance."

The accompanying photo was the same as the one from the missing persons flyer on the corkboard at the police station.

Janet frowned and thought for a beat. Then she Googled "Dr. William Lawter."

Her eyes widened at how many results appeared. Headlines. Photos. Hundreds of search results.

She clicked the link for his "Murderpedia" entry, which she discovered was some kind of Wikipedia for killers. It was sordid, and after just a few minutes perusing the site, she felt like she needed a shower.

Who needs to see all this stuff?

She'd found a trove of information about her former doctor, and as she read, she realized this site was created for someone just like her. Someone looking for answers.

Dr. Lawter was convicted of killing six local people, all adults. He never denied it. When he was finally caught, he'd actually been quite forthcoming with details. What Janet found intriguing was how the writers of his Murderpedia entry explained his motive. He claimed the poisonings were the only way he could end an evil that held Oakport under its sway.

She read from one of the few interviews he'd granted since his trial.

"Interviewer: Do you feel any remorse for your actions? After all, those people had families, and you were supposed to be their caretaker."

"Dr. Lawter: No. Not at all. I have no remorse, just peace of mind. The problem is, I should be seen as a hero. A hero! But at least I'm safe here, and I know I tried my best."

Janet remembered Dr. Lawter for his level-headed demeanor and striking blue eyes. The site had his booking photo. He looked unhinged, a broken shell of his former self. He'd clearly suffered some kind of breakdown since she'd seen him last.

Janet continued to read, biting her thumbnail, until a loud thump from behind the bedroom door startled her.

She held still and listened. When she heard another thump, she set her laptop on the end table and stood. She halfway expected to see the boy in the red jacket staring at her from the kitchen. But nothing was amiss.

She checked the front door and found it still locked.

She went over to her mom's bedroom and eased the door open and leaned inside. Her mom was in bed, arms pointed straight at the ceiling, fists clenched, eyes closed, breathing deeply.

Janet stepped forward, squinting as her eyes adjusted to the dim glow of the night light on the far side of the bed.

Her mother whispered, "Come and see." She then swung her arms back in a casting off gesture, striking the wall above her headboard with a loud thump.

Janet stared, dumbstruck, as her mom reset, again pointing her arms at the ceiling.

"Mom?"

Again, her mom whispered, "Come and see." She again swung her arms back, but Janet grabbed them before she hit the wall.

Janet shook her gently, surprised she'd remained asleep. Her mom's hands were red and swollen from hitting the wall. Her arthritis normally pained her, and to have slept through smashing her hands against the wall was making Janet really start to worry.

"Mom, wake up."

Her mom's eyes flashed open and she sat bolt upright. She seemed shocked to see Janet, and that she was holding her arms down against the bed.

"Oh, Janet… Don't do that." Her mom was flustered, even a bit embarrassed. "What are you doing in here?"

"You were hitting the wall."

Her mom pulled her arms free.

"Well, I'm not now, am I?" Her mom shifted in her bed, agitated. "Some people have trouble sleeping as they get older. Some start talking in their sleep or sleep walking out of the blue."

"Well…" Janet said, worried, "if you need anything, let me know."

"I just need to be left alone." Her mom dropped flat and rolled over to her side.

"Good night."

CHAPTER 7

I.

THE SUN SEEMED too bright this morning. It hurt Janet's eyes as if she had a hangover, but she hadn't had a drink since learning of her pregnancy a month ago. She sat at the dining room table, again watching her mom work at the stove, this time dishing up oatmeal.

Janet smiled weakly as her mom brought the bowls over. "The thing about breakfast for dinner is you don't want it the next morning."

Her mom scoffed, placed a hand on her hip. "I thought you liked oatmeal?"

"Don't you remember anything about what happened last night?"

"When?" she said, sitting down and putting her napkin in her lap.

"When I came into your room."

"What? Why on earth for?"

"You were hitting the wall. And whispering 'Come and see' or something like that."

"Obviously, I was dreaming. They've been coming on strong since your dad's stroke."

"But you spoke to me. So you must have been awake." Janet was starting to wonder if she was remembering things correctly. But the details were so clearly defined in her mind. Her mom had been slamming her hands against the wall, whispering repeatedly.

"Maybe I wasn't. Your father says I sleepwalk sometimes. One time he found me sitting right here, sound asleep, eating a peanut butter and garlic sandwich. I told him it was delicious. But I didn't remember that, either."

Her mom laughed and spooned some oatmeal into her mouth.

2.

WITH HER phone to her ear, Janet left her parents' trailer at Delta Palms and walked toward her car parked in the gravel driveway. She'd called Brian, wanting to update him on what was happening, and to perhaps have a little support, but the conversation wasn't going as planned.

"You're not listening to me," Janet said, exasperated.

"I am listening," Brian said.

Is that condescension in his tone?

"I just don't see how any of this is connected. You had a dream that your doctor killed people?"

"No! He really did kill people. My dream was about the boy I saw in front of the school and in my classroom."

"And you now think he's the ghost of this missing kid?"

"You think I'm crazy, don't you?"

"No. I think you're stressed. I think you should come home."

"I can't just leave. Not now."

"Why not? Isn't that what you did before?" Brian said.

She could hear him pacing in the background. Their apartment seemed so far away. He seemed farther away, as if he was starting to pull free from her.

"I have to go," she said.

"Wait. I'm sorry. That didn't sound the way I meant it to."

"I'll call you later."

Janet ended the call and jammed the phone into her purse. She got into her car and started the engine. Her mom was peering out the window, the curtains pushed aside. She looked old. Frail. She hadn't planned on having to take care of her aging parents. When you're a child, parents were never supposed to become old people. They were supposed to be there at all times, in fine health, supportive and consoling when need be. She learned at a young age that holding on to such a sentiment could only lead to pain and resentment.

Her mom let the curtain fall and came out. With some difficulty from her swollen hands, she locked the trailer, then moved with pained slowness to the car. She opened the passenger side door, sat with a huff, and said nothing.

Janet focused on the road as she pulled away. They shared an awkward silence as she drove out to the house where she'd grown up.

When they arrived, her mom finally spoke. "All the tools and other stuff is in the barn, far as I know. Want me to help look?"

"No. It's okay. You get started in the attic."

Her mom entered the house and Janet headed over to the barn.

Halfway there, she stopped in her tracks. She stared into the endless acres of almond trees, quivering with fear as she saw glimpses from her dream: hearing the baby's cry, tracking the sound into the orchard, then clawing at the dirt until she unburied the arm inside the red jacket. Brushing the dirt from his face…

She listened intently, as if she might again hear the cry carried on the breeze rustling through the orchard. Luckily, she heard no cry. She continued on to the barn, trying to shake free of her dream.

3.

JANET TURNED on a fluorescent light fixture over the workbench and started rummaging around. Her dad had a tool for every purpose, but he wasn't good about organizing them. Covered in a film of sawdust, she came across woodworking tools, crumpled empty cigarette packs, the sketches for a dollhouse he was building for her but never finished. After digging for a few moments, she found a can of putty sitting on a small shelf near the window.

She opened it, not surprised to see it was completely dried out. She sighed, taking the can with her.

When she came out to the driveway, she stopped in her tracks when she saw the Mazda's passenger's side door ajar. A boy was inside. At first, she thought it was the boy in the red jacket, but it was clearly not him. This boy had jet black hair and dark skin. No red jacket in sight. This boy was ransacking her belongings.

No, it wasn't a long-lost boy, it was a thief.

"Hey!" she yelled and trotted over.

It was the boy, Gabriel, she'd found inside her parents' home when she first arrived. He startled at her voice. His eyes bugged out as he looked back at her. He jumped across the seat, opened the driver's door, and hit the ground running, still stuffing her cash into his pants pocket.

Janet paused long enough to see her purse had been dumped out and her wallet had been emptied.

"You little—" She dropped the can of putty and took off after Gabriel, chasing him around the far side of the house. "Come back here right now!"

Gabriel cut through the trees like an expert, switching rows and jumping over the irrigation berms.

Despite being an adult who kept in shape, Janet had a hard time keeping up, and Gabriel soon disappeared through a wall of brush at the back of the orchard.

Janet emerged through the brush and stopped, staring at the vine-covered ruins of a house set behind barbed wire fencing. She felt an overpowering sense of déjà vu. The house was old, looking to be at least one hundred and fifty years old. It was uninhabitable, but it had once been opulent. It had a stone wall surrounding what would've once been a sprawling garden, and a deep porch with broad windows that were mostly shattered. Sections of the roof had caved in, and scorch marks marring the walls indicated a fire had long ago swept through the place.

She marveled at this strange discovery. She had never been here before, at least not that she could ever remember, yet something about the house was so familiar.

Rusted "NO TRESPASSING" signs hung at odd angles from the barbed wire fencing.

What is this place?

Something caught her eye—a flash of white moving behind a collapsed section of wall.

"Hey! You're not supposed to be in there. It's dangerous." Janet stepped closer to the fence. "Just give me the money back and I won't tell anyone!"

Gabriel peeked over the wall's edge, then ducked again.

Janet found a collapsed section of fence and stepped over it, careful to avoid the barbed wire. She headed for a low flight of stairs that led up to a large patio, the brick cracked and weed-laden.

A fountain was at its center, topped with four angels. Triangular planter boxes sat on each corner, holding dead rose bushes. The sides of the planters facing the patio were curved and covered with arcane symbols. In a strip along the top edge, the words Kommen Sie appeared repeatedly.

Before Janet could take a closer look, Gabriel burst from his hiding spot and ran back toward the orchard.

"Hey!" Janet ran after him. The shortest distance was through a section of the charred ruins, but she avoided it, taking a longer route around instead.

Gabriel disappeared into a dilapidated fifth wheel trailer, slamming the screen door behind him.

Janet reached the trailer a moment later, out of breath, and stopped when saw a Rottweiler. It was chained to the stairs and growled at her, its limbs tense and ready to lunge.

The screen door opened again and a Hispanic man in his forties stepped out, a double-barreled shotgun leaning on his shoulder.

Janet gasped and lifted her hands. "Whoa, whoa!"

"¿Quién es usted?"

"What?"

"Who are you?"

"I'm Wayne's daughter. Janet."

"Who's Wayne?"

"The one you're working for. The owner of the orchard. You're Mr. Martinez, right?"

"Mardinez. With a D."

"Mardinez, sure. Sorry."

"You can call me Facundo." He lowered the shotgun and leaned it against the door frame. Janet noticed Gabriel in the shadows behind the screen door. "And that's your son, Gabriel?"

Facundo rolled his eyes and glanced at Gabriel. "What did he do this time?"

"He stole money from my purse," Janet said. "It was in my car."

"¿Es eso cierto?"

"No!" Gabriel said emphatically.

"Ven y vacía tus bolsillos. Ahora!"

Gabriel slowly exited the trailer. Facundo stared at him, waiting.

"¡Darse prisa!"

Gabriel removed the money out of his pocket.

Facundo grunted in anger and snatched the money away from him. "Lo siento." He handed the money to Janet. "I'm sorry. It won't happen again."

Janet took the money. "I'm sure it won't," she said, still looking at Gabriel. "Gracias."

"De nada."

As she walked back through the orchard and the barn came into view, it surprised her to see an Oakport police car parked behind hers. After picking up the can of putty she'd dropped when she spotted Gabriel, she heard voices coming from the open first-floor window.

"Skovil doesn't know anything about it," a man's gruff voice said. "He's in the dark, and I plan on keeping it that way."

Her mom clucked her tongue, then replied, "How can you be sure?"

Mom, who are you talking to?

"Because I am."

Janet slinked toward the open window, hoping to hear more, just as Chief Keegin and her mom exited through the mudroom door.

"There you are," her mom said.

"What's going on? Is Dad okay?"

"Harry's here about yesterday." Her mom cocked an eyebrow. "You know. Your little visit to the police station? All those questions you asked?"

"Did I do something wrong?" Janet asked, turning to Keegin.

"No. Officer Skovil said you seemed very upset when you left." Keegin rocked forward on his feet.

He was lying, Janet could tell. "Of course I was."

"That got me worried. I thought I should check on you. Make sure you weren't going to do anything rash."

"Like what?" Janet said, her anger rising.

"Like drive your car into the river again. What do you think?" her mom said.

"Now, Doris—"

"Don't 'Now, Doris' me, Harry," she cut in. "It's why you're here, isn't it?"

"No. I'm fine," Janet said. "I'm well beyond anything like that. That was a long time ago."

"Good to hear. Isn't it, Doris?" Keegin said.

Her mom looked from Keegin to Janet. "If it's the truth."

"Well…I'll let you two get back to it. House is looking very nice, by the way."

Chief Keegin tipped his hat to both of them, then got in his car and drove out.

"Why did you want to see those reports?" her mom asked.

"I told you what my doctor said." Janet felt defensive. "I thought it would help."

"Help what?"

"Help me deal with it," Janet said.

"That's the only reason?"

"Of course. Why else?"

"I'd hate to think it was because you didn't believe me."

"Why would you lie about a thing like that?"

"Exactly. Why would I?"

Her mom started back toward the house.

Janet stared after her for a beat, then glanced at the can of putty in her hand. "I have to go into town."

"For what?" Her mom looked back.

"Putty. This can is useless, all dried out. Those nail holes need to be sealed or damp will get in the walls. You need anything?"

"Yeah. A pitcher of margaritas."

Without waiting for a reply, her mom turned away and went inside.

Janet tossed the can of putty on the passenger seat, then gathered the scattered contents of her purse. She tossed a lipstick, assorted old receipts, and a tin of breath mints into the waiting maw of her purse. She hadn't thought to lock her door. It was silly to think she would ever have to lock her car in her parents' driveway in the outskirts of sleepy Oakport.

What's the world coming to?

She came across Dr. Gossett's business card on the floor. She considered the phone number, wondering if she should give her a call. A lot was happening. Perhaps she needed a sounding board. Dr. Gossett had insisted it was fine to call her at any time.

She flipped it over, again reading what Gossett had written there in her perfect script: The treasure you seek is in the cave you fear to enter.

She flicked the card with an index finger, nodding, liking the handwritten words even more. She put the card back in her wallet, started the engine, and pulled away.

4.

JANET PARKED in front of the hardware store and got out. During the drive, she kept thinking about her fear, wondering how she could face it. She'd been on the run from her fear ever since she left town. That act in itself was the first act of avoidance in a laundry list that had guided her adult life. She wouldn't find any answers until she confronted that fear.

On her way to the entrance of the hardware store, she glanced across the street, at the bright yellow sandwich board outside Bob's Books.

She veered away from the hardware store and entered Bob's. She remembered this store well. It felt and smelled like it hadn't change a bit over the years. Sitting behind the counter, Bob himself greeted her with a warm smile. He was an old man now, but he'd always seemed old to her.

"Can I help you, young lady?"

She didn't see recognition in his eyes, for which she was grateful. Her time in Oakport had ended in notoriety, and for once she felt like she could pass through in a veil of anonymity.

"True crime books?" she said, even though she had a pretty good idea where to start looking.

"Sure thing. Right this way!"

She followed Bob down an aisle between floor-to-ceiling shelves packed with used books.

"Always the pretty ones want true crime." He glanced at her over his shoulder. "That or cookbooks."

Ugh…Bob, you creepy perv. "Is that so?"

"Yep. You'd be amazed. Only the dogs read romance."

Janet tried to hide her disgust at his unguarded sexism. He was trying to compliment her, which made it even worse.

"There a particular case you're interested in?"

"Yes. A local one."

"Must be Dr. Lawter."

"That's right."

"Lucky you. I'm interested in that one, too."

At the end of the aisle, Bob pointed proudly at an endcap display featuring framed newspaper clippings and paperback books under Lawter's mugshot. Above it all, a sign read "Oakport's Own 'Lawter the Slaughterer.' "

Bob smiled, proud of himself. "Came up with the nickname myself."

"Did you?"

Bob ran an index finger along the titles, pulled one from the rest. He handed it to Janet.

"This one's the best, in my honest opinion."

"Hello?" a woman called out from among the labyrinthine aisles. "I need some help finding a title."

Bob sighed, irritated by the interruption. "Excuse me."

He squeezed past Janet and headed to the front of the shop.

Janet stared at the book he'd handed her, then traded it for one with a less lurid cover. After a few minutes, Janet went to the register, and set the book on the counter.

He motioned toward the aisle behind her with his chin. "See. I told you."

Janet looked back and saw a middle-aged woman in an ill-fitting lime-green pantsuit browsing the romance section.

Bob tapped away on his ancient cash register. "Five dollars even."

Janet forced a smile as she handed him the money. "No thanks," she said as he started to bag her purchase. She took the book and exited, feeling his gaze follow her until she was out of view.

5.

JANET HAD almost forgotten about the real reason for her visit to town—the putty—and rushed inside the hardware store. When she returned to her car, she decided to take the long way back to the house, detouring so she could drive past Dainty's.

She slowed when she saw Ethan carrying trash bags around to the dumpster. He glanced up as she passed. She froze for a moment, and then recognition dawned on his face. He was still quite handsome, more so even. She immediately ducked low so she could barely see over the steering wheel, then sped away.

In her rearview mirror, Ethan had turned to face her retreat. He looked like a lost little boy.

CHAPTER 8

I.

JANET SAT IN her car parked in front of her parents' house. She didn't want to face her mom. Not right now. She thought about just pulling back out and driving…well, just about anywhere else.

She saw the book about Dr. Lawter sitting on the passenger's seat. She grabbed it, opened it, and started reading. It was shlocky and written at a low-grade level, but it was also riveting. It didn't take long to read a dozen or more pages. Finally, when she reached a chapter with the heading, Moloch, she slowed down, taking in every detail, sometimes rereading whole paragraphs.

She flipped forward to the photo section. On the first page was a picture of Dr. Lawter being arrested by Sheriff Keegin. On the next page was a picture of Moloch, represented as a giant bull with seven doors in his chest. The caption read: "Moloch (also spelled Molech) is a Biblical name for a Canaanite god associated with child sacrifice. These sacrifices were undertaken in order to guarantee good harvests or to protect from outsiders."

Below this was an illustration labeled "Sigil of Moloch" which looked like an H made of crosses joined with an M. She recognized this symbol. She'd seen it on the planter boxes at the burned-out house on her family's land.

Janet lifted her head, unable to believe she'd found a connection like this. Lawter was somehow connected to the mythological Moloch, which was tied to her family's orchard.

She closed the book, took her phone with her, and got out of the car. She made sure to lock it this time before heading over to the orchard. She followed the path she had earlier, when she chased Gabriel.

Janet stepped over the downed section of barbed wire fence and ascended the steps to the patio of the burned-out house.

She approached the fountain in the center and looked at the four angels more closely. Each of them carried a banner with their name written in ornate script: Gabriel, Uriel, Michael, and Raphael. Each of them was also pointing in a different direction, like a compass.

She crouched next to the first planter box and searched the symbols on its face until she found the one that matched the "Sigil of Moloch" from the book.

She held the book open next to the symbol, then used her phone to take a side-by-side picture. She then snapped a picture of the words repeated in the strip along the top edge: Kommen Sie. Kommen Sie.

"Hey!" her mom yelled somewhere close. "Get out of there!"

Startled, Janet jerked her head around. Her mom stood beyond the fence line.

Janet hid the book in the planter box and stood. "What's the problem?"

"Trying to break your leg again?"

"What?" Janet said, stepping away from the fountain.

"Don't tell me you forgot about that, too."

"What is this place?"

"It's the original house. Your dad's great-grandpa, Johann, built it after coming over from Germany. When it burned down, the family built the Victorian on the other side of the orchard."

"He must've been wealthy."

"He was, indeed. From owning the land on which he planted this orchard, to having to fight off the native Miwuk when he first set eyes on the place, that all took money. Johann's father had made a fortune innovating some kind of manufacturing technique back in Germany, but your great-great-grandfather didn't want to follow in his shadow. So, he came here with his young wife, Marianna, along with enough money to buy the gunmen to clear the natives."

"And my broken leg?" she asked, but small details were bubbling to the surface, details she didn't want to come into full focus.

"You went exploring the old house, got turned around. You fell somehow, broke your leg."

Janet faced the house, overcome by a sudden wave of emotion. Pain throbbed in her leg just below her knee. She stumbled, as if her leg was once again freshly broken.

"Janet…" her mom said, her voice drifting away. "Are you okay? Maybe you should—"

She blinked as the sky went black and she fell, or seemed to fall, down a limitless chasm. As she fell, the earth itself opened up and she…

She was screaming, having lost all sense of where she was.

When she opened her eyes, she lay sprawled in a blanket of burned debris, a landscape of cold cinders and blown ash. The moon gleamed through a charred window in the dark backdrop of night, making the burned parts of the house look as if they were laced with ice.

She didn't know how she had gotten here. The last thing she remembered…the last thing…her father. Yes, he had chased her here.

He was close by and angry.

"Janet!" her dad yelled. "You shouldn't be in there. It's not safe."

Neither is being near you. She pushed away into the corner of the room, trying to seem as small as possible, trying to become invisible.

She remembered now, though all she wanted to do was forget, to push the memory so deep down inside her that it would be like it had never happened.

She'd been soundly asleep when she'd felt a calloused hand caressing her thigh. She'd screamed when her eyes opened to her dad's lecherous stare. His hand had crept high, under her nightgown. She'd raked her fingers across his face, then ran. Ran so very hard. Like her life depended on it.

She remembered not only the feel of his rough paw on her flesh, but the intent of that contact. Shuddering, she felt like vomiting.

A door creaked nearby. His boots crushed the cinders as he came inside.

"Janet, come out now, and let's talk this over."

When she wiped sweat from her brow, she noticed how her hands were black with soot. Almost invisible in the middle-of-night darkness. Quickly, she rubbed her hands along the charred walls, the ash debris beneath her. She then rubbed her arms and legs, then her face, then her nightgown.

"Hiding only makes it worse," her dad said, closer.

Peeking around the corner into the next room, she saw her dad, but not how she pictured him. In her mind's eye, he was old, enfeebled. He'd fallen off the ladder, suffered a stroke. This man was young, his movements as he searched the house, fluid and strong.

No, he could never be old and broken down. He would always be this monster.

As she pulled away from the doorway, her hand brushed a cinder, sending it skittering a few feet. She pressed a hand to her mouth to stifle a gasp.

"Oh, so this is the game we're playing. Hide-and-seek."

She froze when his boots strode by just feet away. A beat later, he entered the burned husk of a room, his silhouette like a black hole.

"Come on, now, girlie." He opened a Zippo and sparked it to life, squinting against the brightness for a moment before putting his free hand between his face and the flame. The flickering orange light made every shadow look like a black curtain blowing in the breeze. "Quit this nonsense and come back to the house with me."

He stepped forward, moving the lighter back and forth, then lifting it high over his head.

Janet held her breath as the orange light moved toward her like encroaching flood water.

"Found you, girlie," he said. "I was going to be nice about this, thinking we might be able to forget anything ever happened."

"Leave me alone!" she shouted, her voice sounding incredibly small in the vastness of the house.

Smirking, he squatted down in front of her, backing her into a corner. She looked for a place to run to, but there was no place to go. He reached for her legs, and she kicked at him, which elicited a throaty chuckle from him.

Lunging lightning-quick, he took hold of her nightgown with both fists. She cried out, terrified, but this only seemed to energize him and he yanked her close, tearing the fabric. The exposed skin of her upper thighs was bone white against the ash staining the rest of her. His amusement became a full, unabashed laughter.

Janet leapt away, but he was too quick.

After catching her throat in one meaty fist, he slammed her to the ground, grunting with the effort. In the violent motion, her leg caught under her. Her leg twisted until a bolt of pain exploded just below her knee, followed by the nauseating sound of snapping bone. She let out a shriek, and then his boot slammed into her temple. She blinked, saw him squatting closer to her, a wide smile across his lips, nothing but menace in his eyes. And then all became as dark as the cinders under foot.

2.

WHEN JANET opened her eyes, she was on a couch under a blanket.

Then she noticed a dog licking her hand, and she pulled it away fast. It was the Rottweiler she'd seen earlier. The orchard keeper's dog. The Rottweiler. Facundo. Yes, Facundo was the orchard keeper.

Across the room, Gabriel got up from a chair and opened the accordion door into the kitchen. "Ella esta despierta ahora."

The boy stepped back and his father entered. Janet pushed the blanket off and sat up.

"How did I get here?" she said groggily. Her mind flashed to sound of her nightgown tearing, to the feeling of her leg twisted under her until it snapped.

"Tu madre," Facundo said. "She said you fall down. She asked me to bring you here."

"Where is she?" She sat up a little higher. "Where's my mom?"

"Gone. For help. The police, I think."

"Doctor, you mean."

"I don't know. But she said you have to stay. If you wake up, you can't go."

"No," Janet said. "It's okay. I'm fine. Really. I need to let her know that." She patted her pockets for her phone, but it wasn't there. She stood and turned around, searching the couch cushions. "Do you know where my phone is?"

"No," Facundo replied. "I never saw it."

"Did you take it?" she asked Gabriel.

"No," the boy said.

"I have to go now."

"No. Please. She made me promise."

"You don't want the police to come here if they don't need to, do you? They won't be happy about that." She was starting to feel less groggy. More like herself. "And you don't want to make the police unhappy."

"No," Facundo said in a low voice.

"Okay, then. Let me go find my mother so I can tell her everything is fine. All right?"

"Déjala ir. Ella es problema," Gabriel said.

"Problema?" Janet said. "What is? What's a problem?"

"No. It's okay," Facundo said. "Go."

Facundo and Gabriel followed Janet outside. She glanced over her shoulder, and they watched grimly as she hurried into the orchard.

When she reached the patio of the burned house, she ascended the steps and looked for the book she'd hidden in the planter box.

It was gone.

She searched the other planter boxes, but to no avail. She checked the ground for any sign of her phone.

What the hell?

At a loss, Janet stared at the house. After gathering her courage, she started to walk toward the front door.

When she entered the front room, she felt a huge surge of déjà vu. She'd been here as a young girl, and she'd hidden in the charred remains of the building because…because her dad had been chasing after her.

She knew her way around the house. This wasn't any simple case of déjà vu. She'd really been here, and that part of her memory was a murky recess she couldn't quite see into. It was those buried memories that compelled her feet forward, back outside to where the cellar entrance was. The doors were open.

Janet approached cautiously, peering over the edge. Wooden stairs descended to a pool of solid darkness. Halfway down the stairs, between the top and the shadows below, she spotted her phone.

How did that get here?

Reluctantly, Janet crossed the threshold. The wood creaked ominously as she stepped onto the top stair. She moved down to the second step…then the third. On the fourth step, she crouched. As she reached for her phone, she noticed movement in the darkness below. Movement accompanied by a skittering noise.

Like liquid, the inky black rose, covering the steps in irregular patterns.

With her heart racing, Janet grabbed her phone and raced back up the steps.

The darkness behind her spilled over the threshold and flowed down to the ground in a spreading pool.

Eyes wide with fear, Janet ran as fast as she could, across the patio, and into the orchard. She left the burned-out house behind, sprinting through the orchard, across the undulating irrigation berms.

Covered in sweat, Janet reached her parents' barn and hugged the wall, moving toward the edge carefully before peeking around the corner.

She saw her mom and Chief Keegin exiting the rear of the house.

"We'll get there faster if we drive," Keegin said. "What if she wakes up, starts talking?"

"We'll deal with it as it comes," her mom replied, her tone icy.

They got into the police car and sped toward the dirt road on the far side of the property and Facundo's trailer.

Janet ducked back and waited until the car was out of sight before entering the barn. She knew exactly what she had to do. She didn't want to, but she saw no other option.

After grabbing a shovel and a crowbar, she felt a bit surer of herself with their heft in her hands. She tossed the tools into the backseat of her car and got in. As she drove into town, she slowed as she approached Dainty's. Not wanting to be seen, she turned into the alley around back, finding an empty spot near the dumpsters.

3.

SHE SAT in the car, nearly hyperventilating, and if she wasn't careful, she'd tip over into a full-on panic attack. Closing her eyes, she tried to shut out the burnt smell from the house next to the orchard, tried to push out thoughts of Dr. Lawter, his many supposed victims, the strange connections to Moloch. This was how, she realized, she would have to confront her fear. Only by confronting her fear would she overcome her past. But in order to overcome her past, she had to first unbury it. And that unburial had to begin with her talking to Ethan.

Jesus, Dr. Gossett. Is this the only way?

What finally calmed her nerves was the image of Brian smiling. She touched her still-flat belly, knowing that something made of both of them was growing inside her. Opening her eyes, she glanced at the shovel and crowbar in the back seat. She wondered what attention she'd bring upon herself if she brought them with her.

Come on, Janet, you can do this. You have to do this.

She let out one long, calming breath, then got out of the car went around to the front of the diner. A bell rattled above the door as she entered. A waitress looked up from behind the counter, where she was refilling a patron's water glass.

"Just one?" The waitress walked around the counter, grabbing a menu from the caddy as she went.

"I'm sorry?" Janet said, distracted.

"Table for one?"

"No. I'm looking for Ethan."

"He expecting you?

Janet saw Ethan through the serving window, putting a plate under the hot lights. He needed a shave. He had a three-day beard, but she supposed it looked good on him.

The waitress looked over her shoulder, said, "This lady's here to see you."

Ethan's eyes locked with Janet's. She didn't know what his reaction would be. A strange look of relief swept over his face, and she let out a tense breath.

"So I'm not going crazy?" Ethan said through the serving window. His smile was still warm, his dimples more defined with age.

"I wouldn't feel so sure," Janet said. "Not with what I have to say."

The waitress glanced back and forth between the two of them for a moment, then returned the menu to the caddy. She took the plate from under the heat lamp to a man seated in a window booth.

Ethan came out from the kitchen through the swinging doors and approached Janet hesitantly. He wiped his hands on the apron at his waist. "You drove by earlier, right? When I was taking the trash out?"

She nodded, feeling like she'd been caught in some illicit act.

"I thought I was seeing things. Nice to know I'm not. You in town because of your dad?"

"No." She hesitated. "Because of Joey."

His face soured, filled with sudden sadness. "What does that mean?"

"I'm sorry. Okay? For everything that happened before. And also for coming in here like this. But I need your help. And you're the only one I can trust. I think. I hope."

"Are you in trouble?"

"Not exactly. It's complicated."

"I'm free in a couple hours. Can we talk then?"

"It can't wait. I'll have to explain on the way."

"On the way where?"

The waitress returned with an order from another table. She clipped it on the wheel next to the hot lights, called out, "Order in."

"Please, Ethan," she said, trying to hide her desperation and failing. "If you don't want to help, just tell me and I'll figure something else out."

"I swear, only you could make twelve years feel like twelve hours."

"Is that a yes?"

"Did you hear me?" the waitress said.

Ethan replied, not looking away from Janet, "Go pull Stan off his break."

The waitress, taken aback by his tone, slammed through the swinging doors into the kitchen. "Stan!"

Ethan untied his apron, said, "Want me to drive?"

4.

"SO I'M guessing we don't have time for small talk?" Ethan said as he followed Janet to her car. "You know, like, where have you been living and what do you do for work?"

"I teach second grade at a private school in San Francisco."

"Married?" he asked with a grin, sounding hopeful she wasn't.

"Almost. But I am six weeks pregnant," she said, stopping in her tracks. His grin disappeared. "Look, Ethan, we can catch up after. But right now, I need you to listen to me. Some of what I'm going to say will sound crazy, but it's not. I swear."

She unlocked the passenger door and opened it. Ethan hesitated, but after one more pleading look from Janet, he got in.

"Okay. We can catch up later. But tell me this…" he lifted one eyebrow, "where to?"

"St. Peter's. We need to go to the cemetery." She held her keys out to him. He hesitated, but grabbed them.

St. Peter's was only a few miles away. Janet used that time to explain what had been happening with her mom, how she had been having strange dreams, how she'd been banging her fists against the wall while chanting "Come and see."

Ethan eased the car to the side of the sleepy road behind the cemetery. A gray stone wall topped with wrought-iron spikes encircled the grounds.

"Okay," he said. "So, your mom's been having weird dreams, and now we're at the cemetery. Now what?"

"Look at this." She handed him her phone, which was open to her saved photos.

"Kommen Sie," he whispered. "What is that?"

"I thought she was saying 'come and see.' But she wasn't."

"She was saying this?"

"Right. 'Kommen Sie.' It's German. It means 'come.' Like a command. Or an invocation."

"But you said she was sleeping."

"Now I'm not so sure. Especially because of the way she was repeatedly hitting the wall. Like it was a pattern, or a ritual. Like she was trying to summon something."

Janet swiped to the next photo: one of the planter box next to the page in the book.

"This is the sigil of Moloch. He's an ancient god associated with child sacrifice."

Ethan nodded, unsure what to think. "Child sacrifice? So, you think that crazy Dr. Lawter wasn't lying?"

"Yes."

"So, you think this Moloch has something to do with Joey?"

Janet's shoulders slumped "You don't believe me, do you?"

"I didn't say that."

"You didn't have to."

"Everything you've said could easily be explained in some other way."

"Not all of it."

"So, what, your parents killed Joey as part of some ritual to this Moloch?"

"Yes. I think they sacrificed our boy in exchange for a good almond crop. They were willing to sacrifice their own grandchild, one which they'd never approved of to begin with, to ensure the health and continuation of the orchard."

Ethan stared, dumbstruck. He shook his head slowly.

"I'm not saying that Moloch is real," Janet said. "I'm saying that's what they believe."

"Okay. But even so, how could you ever prove it? That Lawter guy couldn't. And look where he is."

"That's why I brought you here."

Ethan looked out the window at the wall around the cemetery.

"For what?"

"There's no other choice..." She took a steadying breath. "We need to open Joey's grave."

"What?" He jolted away from her, pressing himself against the door. "No!"

"Yes. If his grave is empty, then it proves all of this is true. It would mean my parents sacrificially killed our little boy. I mean, what other explanation could there be, right?"

"This is madness..." He ran his hands through his hair. He looked like he wanted to open the car door and run away. "What if it isn't empty?"

"Then I'm wrong."

"And we go to jail. I can't do that again, Janet. I'm sorry."

She'd always carried a tremendous guilt that her dad had pressed for statutory rape charges. They'd been in love, but she hadn't been able to sway her dad on the matter. "We won't get caught."

"Isn't that what you said before?" he said, his eyes full of sadness.

"Please, Ethan. If you won't do it for me, at least do it for Joey."

Ethan closed his eyes, squeezed the bridge of his nose. "Jesus..." He looked at her. "Fine. Fine, whatever."

CHAPTER 9

I.

FATHER ROZARO OPEN the Rectory door and smiled when he saw Janet.

"Hello," Rozaro said.

"Can I talk to you?"

"Of course. Come in."

Janet looked over her shoulder as she entered.

Father Rozaro closed the door. He waved for her to follow him down a short hallway. Pastoral paintings lined the walls. Shepherds tending their flocks, mostly. A little on the nose, padre.

"Sorry I didn't call first," she said.

"Don't worry. Most people don't. I was just fixing some tea. Would you like a cup?"

"Yes, please," she said, somewhat relieved.

The surroundings were austere and dated. A worn leather couch was in one corner. A recliner was facing a TV housed in an old wooden case. Bookshelves dominated the space, old tomes with leather bindings. Their smell permeated the air.

The kettle started whistling in the rectory kitchen next to the living room.

"Excuse me." He shuffled into the kitchen and switched off the burner. When he started gathering tea cups, a high-pitched sound suddenly blared.

"Fiddlesticks. Not again. Pardon me for a moment, would you?"

"What is it?" She came over to the kitchen doorway.

"The alarm system. Probably just a cat tripping a motion sensor. But I have to check."

Father Rozaro returned the pot to the burner and exited the kitchen. Janet followed him down a short hallway lined with more paintings of pastoral scenery. He turned into a room. Janet entered a moment later as he crossed the bedroom to a desk on the other side.

He entered a code on a keypad, silencing the alarm, then faced a bank of six five-inch black-and-white monitors. Each displayed a different area of the church buildings and grounds. Ethan was clearly visible on the bottom right screen, carrying a shovel and crowbar.

Father Rozaro gasped. "What the Devil?" He grabbed his glasses from the nightstand and put them on as he leaned in for a closer view.

"What is it, Father?"

"That looks like Ethan Frewel," he said, turning to her. "Doesn't it?"

When Janet didn't answer, Father Rozaro stood and turned around fully.

Janet panicked and hit him on the head with the nearest heavy object—a sculpture of praying hands she'd taken from the dresser.

Father Rozaro stumbled backward, and his eyes rolled back in his head. He tripped over the corner of the bed and fell to the floor, unconscious.

"Oh, Jesus," she whispered, her limbs buzzing with adrenaline, fear, and remorse.

I just clobbered a priest. If there is a Hell, I just bought a one-way ticket.

Janet dropped the sculpture on the bed and patted his pockets for the keys. She found them and took off running toward the cemetery.

2.

WHEN SHE reached Joey's grave, Ethan was on his hands and knees, using the crowbar to clear the grass from the edge of the crypt's lid. As she approached, he jumped to his feet and whirled around.

"It's okay. It's me!" Janet stepped closer.

"God, you nearly gave me a heart attack." He tilted his head. "Where's Father Rozaro?"

"Out cold."

"Is he going to be okay?"

"I hope so." She gestured to the crypt. "Can you do it?"

"I don't know yet. Let me see." Ethan dropped to the ground again. He wedged the hook end of the crowbar under the lid, but it sunk into the grass when he pulled it down. "Use the shovel."

Ethan reset the crowbar, and Janet slid the shovel under it. Ethan pulled back. This time, the crowbar pressed against the shovel and the stone growled as the lid lifted up.

"Push it over!" Ethan said.

Janet left the shovel and threw her weight against the lid, sliding it to one side.

Ethan yanked the crowbar free and dropped it. Then the two of them grabbed the edge of the lid and pulled it backward.

Janet stared into the crypt. The infant-sized casket inside was surprisingly well-preserved.

"Oh, God," Ethan said, short of breath. "It's so small."

"Will you...open it? Please?"

Ethan crouched and grabbed the handle. He looked at Janet. "Are you sure about this?"

"Yes. Hurry! Do it."

Ethan tried to lift the lid, but it was stuck. He hefted the crowbar and used the long end to pry it loose. When it finally pulled free, he dropped the crowbar with a metallic clatter and threw the lid back.

Inside the casket, nestled in a bed of ruffled blue silk, were three red bricks.

"Empty..." Janet gasped and covered her mouth with her hand before she collapsed to the ground.

"Janet..." Ethan said, his voice somehow distant. Before she could say anything else, darkness swept in, blanketing her every word, thought, movement.

3.

JANET'S EYES opened slowly. Her vision was bleary at first, as if she were looking through water-streaked glass. Lightning flashed. The black windows were indeed wet with rain.

She looked to her side, saw an EKG machine, then lifted one hand that had an IV needle taped in place. With her other hand, she fumbled for the call button and pressed it repeatedly until a nurse entered.

"Okay. Okay. I'm here. The doctor is on his way."

"What time is it?" Janet asked, her voice a reedy wisp.

"A little after three."

The nurse took the call button out of Janet's hand and hung it over the side rail of the gatch bed. A doctor entered the room, and the nurse stood up straight.

"Hello. I'm Dr. Tomasulo." He rubbed sleep from his eyes and stifled a yawn. "Can you tell me your name?"

"Don't you know?"

"Yes. But I need to make sure you do. Standard stuff after a head injury like yours."

Janet ran her fingers over the bandages on her scalp.

"Janet. Janet Martlee."

"Good. And what year is it?"

"2020."

"Month?"

"September... No, October."

"Hundred percent. Do you know how you got here?"

Janet shook her head.

"Okay. What's the last thing you do remember?"

Janet hesitated, unsure what to say.

"How about what you had for breakfast?"

"Oatmeal." Janet wrinkled her nose. "I don't like oatmeal."

The doctor grinned. "Good. How about lunch?"

"Nothing. I didn't have time. How long have I been here?"

"About twelve hours."

"Does my mother know?"

"Yes. She's in the waiting area downstairs. With some friends of yours, I think."

"Friends? Who?" She thought about Ethan. Surely, he would've waited for her. But who else would be with him?

"Brian and Angela? Does that sound right?"

"Hmm…" she said, confused. "When did they get here?"

"I only know they were here when I came on at 7:00."

"What about Ethan?"

Dr. Tomasulo took a deep breath and traded an awkward glance with the nurse.

"I'm sorry…but…he didn't survive the accident."

"What…what accident?" She shifted in the bed, wanting to move, to do something.

"You hit a tree and drove into the river."

"No. That's what they said before. After Joey died."

The doctor looked both puzzled and uncomfortable. "I don't know anything about that. Should I get your mother?"

"No!" She pictured her mother chanting, calling on Moloch. Sacrificing her boy. Her baby. My poor Joey.

Dr. Tomasulo seemed shocked by her forcefulness.

"I'm just not feeling up to it," she said, trying to make up an excuse on the fly. God, her head was still thick as pea soup. "Not yet, anyway. Please."

"All right. Let the nurse know when you change your mind. I'll check back in a few hours."

Janet sat a little higher. "When can I leave?"

"Not for a couple of days at least."

"Days?" She sighed. "Really?"

"Head injuries can be tricky. The MRI we took earlier looks good. I have a follow-up scheduled for tomorrow. If that shows no change, we'll talk about getting you home. Until then, rest."

Dr. Tomasulo exited.

The nurse lingered by the door. "Lights on or off?"

"Off, please."

The nurse switched the lights off and left.

Janet waited until the door closed, then took out the nasal cannula and threw the covers back. She scanned the EKG controls, then turned down the volume dial to nothing. She then pulled the IV, leaving the cotton taped in place, and started looking for her clothes. The built-in cabinet and closet were empty. So was the bathroom.

She didn't find a single article of her clothing. In fact, she didn't find any of her personal effects. No purse. No phone. Nothing.

Janet went to the door. She eased it open a crack. The hallway was empty. Dark. Middle of the night quiet. Janet slipped out and eased the door shut behind her.

4.

WHEN SHE heard laughter at the far end of the hall, she moved in the opposite direction.

Janet entered a room at random, moving as quietly as she could. An old man was asleep in the lone bed. She waited until she was sure he wasn't aware of her presence, then tiptoed to the nightstand. Inside the top drawer, she found clothes: pants, tennis shoes, a shirt, and a hoodie. She pulled the pants on. They were too big, but they would have to do.

After yanking the string out of the hoodie, she threaded it through the belt loops, and tied it in a knot. She took off the hospital gown and slipped the shirt on. Then the hoodie, and finally, the shoes.

She pulled the hood over her head and tucked her hair inside.

The man in the bed let out a weak snore. His skin was pale gray, his lips dry and cracked. The stubble on his cheeks was bushy and would soon need shaving. He looked sickly, like he might never leave this place. She saw no sign that he'd ever been visited—no flowers or get-well cards, no card games waiting to be resumed come tomorrow. Her heart ached as she considered the fact she was stealing from this man, but she wouldn't let guilt sidetrack her.

Glancing at the mirror by the door, she didn't recognize herself.

She sucked in a deep breath and put her ear to the door. She forced her pulse to slow as she opened the door. All clear.

Janet exited the room, went around the corner, and headed for the stairwell.

The doorway opened to the waiting area. She lurked in the shadows, pausing before moving closer to the couches. She stood behind a pillar, peered around the edge of it. Her mom was asleep on a couch, breathing deeply. Brian and Angela were in a row of orange plastic chairs against the opposite wall. Brian was awake, sitting up straight, but with his eyes fixed and glazed as he stared at a TV showing a local weather report. Angela was asleep, her head resting on his shoulder.

When the TV went to commercial, Brian got up carefully, trying not to wake her.

Angela stirred anyway, opening one eye. "Where are you going?"

"Bathroom. Sorry."

She closed her eye again as Brian walked down the hall, his treads loud in the stillness. As soon as he disappeared around the corner, Janet left the shadows of the pillar, pulled the hoodie low over her face, and crouched next to Angela.

She whispered, "Angela."

"Hmm?"

"It's Janet."

"Janet's in the hospital," Angela muttered.

Janet's mom shifted on the couch. She was facing them now, but her eyes remained closed. Janet squeezed Angela's shoulder.

"Come on," Janet said softly. "Wake up. Please."

Angela's eyes fluttered open. When she saw Janet, she startled and sat up fast. Her purse fell to the ground loud enough to make Janet's mom stir again.

When Angela opened her mouth to speak, Janet clamped her hand over her lips.

She leaned close, whispering, "Just come with me."

Janet picked up Angela's purse from the floor. She handed it to her, and they went together down the hall.

"Angela?" Janet's mom called out. "Brian?"

They froze in their tracks, and Janet stepped behind a pillar. Angela looked back over her shoulder.

"Where are you going?" Janet's mom said, bleary-eyed.

"To get a snack," Angela said. "Want anything?"

"Yeah. Cheetos and a Diet Coke."

"Okay. Be right back."

Angela started walking again, and Janet joined her when her mom dropped back to the couch with a sigh.

CHAPTER 10

I.

NOT WANTING TO be seen, they hurried down the stairwell and exited into a dark night left sodden by the passing storm. The air was lush with fragrance from the surrounding trees. The clouds had pushed away, revealing a full moon. Raindrops covered the cars in the parking lot, looking like glowing embers under the sodium vapor lamps.

Angela looked around. They were alone. "Can't you just tell me?"

"You have to see it for yourself. Otherwise you won't believe anything else I say."

"The doctor said I shouldn't anyway. He said a head injury like yours can cause all kinds of problems. Changes in behavior. Hallucinations."

Janet scoffed. "Belief in paranoid conspiracies?"

"That's exactly what he said."

"Of course, it is. He must be in on it, too. We better hurry."

"What about Dr. Gossett?"

"What about her?"

"She said the same thing."

"When did you talk to her?"

"Yesterday. After Brian called me. He was worried because of what you said about that dream you had. I wanted to know what she thought. That's why we're here. She said we should bring you home right away. But the accident happened before we got here."

"There was no accident," Janet said, but she could see in Angela's expression that she didn't believe anything Janet was saying.

"Are you listening to yourself?"

"Did you see the car? Did you see Ethan's body?"

"No."

"Then how can you be sure?"

"The chief of police told us."

"And you believe him over me?"

"In this situation…yes."

"You'll change your mind after you see what I have to show you."

Janet grabbed the keys from Angela and started clicking the fob.

"Hey, wait a minute…" Angela said, trailing off.

Janet didn't care. She had to get out of here, with or without Angela.

"Hold on. Don't leave. Show me. Show. Me."

When Angela's car responded with a chirp-chirp, Janet threw her the keys and got in. After a beat, Angela joined her.

As Angela drove to the exit of the parking lot, Janet watched the street signs.

"Left here." Janet pointed.

Angela made the turn. Within a few minutes the steep slate roof and narrow bell tower of Saint Peter's church loomed into view ahead.

"Okay. Slow down," Janet said.

As Angela eased off the gas, they saw an Oakport police car parked in front of the rectory.

Janet gripped Angela's forearm. "Speed up!"

"You just told me to slow down."

Janet reached down and pushed Angela's knee, making her go faster. After they passed the church, Janet looked through the rear windshield.

"Do you think he saw us?"

"Are you kidding?" Angela said, incredulous. "I can't believe he's not pulling me over."

"This means they know everything. They've probably got it all cleaned up. Put back in place."

"What are you talking about?" Angela said. "You were going to show me, well, now it looks like you have to tell me. Spill it. What's going on, Janet?"

"Joey's grave. I opened it. Ethan helped me. He wasn't in there."

"Who wasn't?"

"Joey. There were only bricks inside his coffin. Ethan sneaked into the cemetery. I had to hit Father Rozaro on the head."

"But Father Rozaro was at the hospital a few hours ago. Your mom asked him to come see you. He seemed fine to me."

Janet widened her eyes and covered her mouth. "Oh, no." She felt defeated.

"What? Now you think he's in on it, too? Whatever 'it' is."

"But he has to be. All of them. They all killed Joey."

"You think that priest murdered your baby?"

"Sacrificed. To Moloch. Put him in the pit of bones and let him die."

"What pit of bones?" Angela said. "You're really starting to worry me, Janet."

Janet thought for a moment. "That's it!" she muttered. "It has to be…"

"What has to be?"

"The bones. They must be at Johann's house. The first house. In the cellar."

Angela lips started to curve in a smile, then stopped "Holy shit. You're serious."

"Take me to the orchard. There's a dirt road leading to a secluded house. It's in ruins. My boy is there. I need to find my boy."

"No. We're going back to the hospital." Angela shook her head. "I should've never let you talk me into taking you away from there."

"Take me to the orchard. Now!"

Angela flinched. She turned slowly, staring at Janet.

"Please," Janet said, the strength leaving her voice. "My Joey is there."

They stared at one another until Angela had to look back to the road. "Okay, Janet…okay. We'll check it out. But no matter what happens, no matter what we see, I think you need help."

2.

THE HEADLIGHTS of the car panned the trees on either side of the driveway leading to Janet's childhood home. Angela kept driving, pulling into the dirt road at the far side of the property.

"It's just around that bend," Janet said.

When the headlights washed over Facundo's trailer, a light went on inside.

"There's a trailer on the property?" Angela asked.

"Yeah, that's for the groundskeeper."

"Is that where that boy lives? The one you caught creeping around your parents' house?"

"Yeah, and I didn't even get to tell you; I found him stealing money from my wallet when I'd left my purse in the car out front."

"Nice neighbors," Angela said, trying to liven the mood.

"Yeah, so nice they'll murder a baby." The enormity of what they were facing seemed to fill the car. "Just pull over near the brush."

"I don't think I have a choice." The headlights revealed that the road ended in a pile of mulch dumped for use in the orchard.

"We'll have to walk from here."

Angela pulled over and set the brake.

When she turned the headlights off, Janet sucked in a breath. "Do you have a flashlight?"

"Hold on." Angela dug her phone out of her purse and turned on the flashlight app. "It's not much, but it's better than nothing."

"Follow me." Janet paused at the fence, staring at the burned house in the moonlight. Angela joined her.

"What is this place?" Angela asked in a whisper.

"It's the original family house. When it burned down, they built the Victorian on the other side of the property." Janet turned to look Angela in the eye. "Do you remember me breaking my leg?"

"In fifth grade. Of course. Why?"

"I didn't," Janet said. "Not until today."

"But Janet…"

"I was standing right up there. My mom was telling me to get out. And she asked me if I was trying to break my leg again. And then it all came back to me. And I mean everything." Janet's stomach roiled.

"What did?"

"That my father…did things to me. Things a father shouldn't do. And he broke my leg doing them."

"I know." Angela's face blanched at the thought.

"What do you mean, you know?"

"You told me. When it happened. When we were kids."

"I did? Jesus, what's wrong with me?"

"I wanted to go to the police. You didn't. And then you made me swear to never talk about it again. That's why I was so worried about you coming back here. But I didn't know how to say it. Not without saying it."

"Then you believe me?"

"About that?" Angela winced. "Of course."

"It happened here. My broken leg…the other stuff. In that burned out house," Janet said. "The rest of it's true, too."

Angela's shoulders slumped as Janet turned away to search for the downed section of fence.

"Where are you going?"

"Up there."

"For what?"

"To prove it to you."

Janet ascended the steps to the patio. She stopped at the fountain and waited for Angela to catch up.

3.

SHE POINTED at the planter boxes. "See that? Those are called sigils. That one's for Moloch."

Angela crouched for a closer look.

Janet pointed to the words. "Kommen Sie. Those words are the invocation, the same invocation I heard my mom chanting in her sleep."

"Is that German?"

"Yes. My great-great-grandfather came here from Germany. Before California was a state. He took this land from the Miwuk. When they tried to take it back, he asked Moloch for protection. And all Moloch asked for in return was a sacrifice."

Janet headed toward the house. "It's been going on ever since. You should see all the missing persons flyers at the police station."

Angela's face creased with worry.

Janet went around the far side of the house and stopped near the open cellar doors.

When Angela joined her, Janet pointed into the darkness.

"It's down there. The pit of bones. Where they put their sacrifices. That's where they put Joey."

"Oh, Janet…" Angela said, sorrowfully.

"I know you don't believe me. But you will. Come on."

"I'm not going down there." Angela shook her head. "Guaranteed there are hordes of spiders and centipedes and rats."

"I'm going. I have to. Otherwise I'll never be free."

"Free from what?"

"From what's happening to me. This is what Dr. Gossett was talking about. She didn't know exactly what it was, but this is what she meant." Janet stepped over the threshold and waited.

Angela hesitated. Janet thought she looked like she didn't want to go down into the cellar, but she probably didn't to want to stay up here in the burned out remains by herself, either.

"Can I at least use your phone?"

"Ugh…you owe me, big time." Angela switched on the flashlight app and handed it to her.

They descended the stairs without incident and reached the floor at the bottom. The space was so large the flashlight app couldn't reach the walls in any direction ahead of them.

"So where is it?" Angela said. "Where is this pit of bones?"

"Must be in the floor somewhere." Janet panned the light across immediate vicinity. She moved forward, sweeping the light across the dirt. Behind her, Angela waited in the weak pool of moonlight shining down the stairs, watching as Janet moved back and forth through the darkness.

"Find anything yet?" Angela said, her voice shaking.

Janet didn't answer.

"I'll take that as a 'no.' "

Angela waited for a response. Seconds passed. The silence became weighty. Impenetrable. The flashlight became fainter as Janet moved farther into the cellar.

"Come on, Janet. Let me take you back to the hospital. Better yet, I'll take you home. Then you can talk to Dr. Gossett about this."

Janet gasped. On the far corner of the room the flashlight revealed an ancient wooden door in the floor. "Come here and hold this for me."

Angela stepped away from the moonlight, into the darkness.

When she reached Janet, she was already on her knees, raking her fingers along the crack around the doorframe.

"Here, take it."

Angela took the phone from her and Janet was now able to use both hands, tracing the square outline.

"Is that a...a door?" The flashlight juddered in Angela's hands.

"Yes. It's a door."

Janet brushed the dirt, uncovering the hinges. She pushed away more dirt and revealed a rusted iron ring. She grabbed it, climbed to her feet, and tugged with all her strength. The hinges gave off a mournful creaking, and then the door was opening, dirt sliding off to the side, stirring up dust clouds like rising smoke.

"My...God." Angela coughed and waved at the dust caught in the flashlight's beam and stepped back.

"I knew it." Janet glanced back at her. Her friend looked like she wanted to run far from here. She didn't blame her. If she didn't have her own reasons for being here, this would be the last place she'd choose to be. "Give me the light."

Angela handed the phone to her.

Janet shined it into the darkness below the door. She picked up a clod of dirt. It felt solid in her hand. She leaned over the hole, still unable to see the bottom, and dropped the clod.

Two seconds later, they heard a distant thump.

And then they heard a second thump, louder than the first.

Janet looked up at Angela. Angela looked toward the ceiling.

"What was that?" Janet said.

"That sounded like it came from upstairs," Angela said, her voice trembling.

"Shh!"

Another thump, definitely from overhead, followed by a chorus of whispering. "Kommen Sie… Kommen Sie…" Each pair of words were punctuated by another thump.

Janet saw Angela look over her shoulder. Shifting shapes at the top of the stairs blocked the moonlight, casting long shadows on the dirt floor.

Janet stood, her muscles tensing. Angela said nothing.

And then they descended the stairs, their feet stomping in a rhythmic, ritualistic thumping. Their faces appeared in the light: Janet's mom, Father Rozaro, Chief Keegin, as well as other people Janet didn't recognize. A dozen or more in total.

"Kommen Sie…" they said as one.

Stomp. Thump.

"Kommen Sie…"

Stomp. Thump.

Janet looked for an escape route. All she saw was darkness. She yelled, "Run!"

Janet ran and Angela followed.

The crowd of people stormed after them in a big wave, still chanting and stomping.

The light finally revealed a wall and Janet followed it to a second stairway to the first floor. She charged at them, taking two at a time, Angela close on her heels.

A gunshot resounded in the enclosed space. Janet looked back, saw Chief Keegin with his revolver still raised, smoke trailing in a thin ribbon from the barrel.

He fired again. In the split-second of brightness from the muzzle-flash, Janet saw Angela's side pop like a blood-filled balloon. She cried out and fell in a heap on the stairs.

"Angela!" Janet started back down the stairs.

Angela shook her head, tears trailing down her cheeks. She held her wound with both hands, blood gushing between her fingers. "No, Janet! Run!"

Chief Keegin fired again and the wood near Janet's head exploded in splinters. Janet fought back a sob—locking eyes with Angela for a split second—and then ducked as she ran up the rest of the steps. In that brief moment, she saw Angela's life draining away.

4.

JANET RAN up the stairs and found herself in the remains of the kitchen. She headed for a door, tried the knob, but it wouldn't budge.

Panicked, she saw a gaping hole in the wall. She heard the sounds of pursuit as she climbed through the opening as fast as she could.

Janet suddenly realized she'd been here before, as a child. It was the room she'd dreamt about. The one in which her father…

She couldn't let herself remember. Not when people were chasing her.

Voices raged behind her as she raced across the patio. They were still chanting, still thumping even as they pursued her.

When she reached the fence, she was in such a panic, she couldn't find the downed section she used to cross over into the ruins. She grabbed the barbed wire to climb over, but her hand slipped, and a barb cut her wrist.

With a pained grunt, she dropped to the ground and slid under the fence, the barbs poking her, snagging her clothes.

Once she was clear of the fence, she got to her feet and sprinted toward the wall of brush. Before she could reach it, Facundo pushed through from the opposite side, double-barrel shotgun in one hand, flashlight in the other.

Janet froze, unsure if she could trust him.

He raised the light toward her face. "Que está pasando?"

Before she could say anything in response Chief Keegin fired his gun and the flashlight shattered.

Janet ducked reflexively as a second gunshot hit Facundo in the shoulder. He howled in pain, spinning backward, the shotgun falling to the dirt a second before he did.

Janet dove toward the weapon, lifted it to a low angle, and pushed the butt into the dirt.

Chief Keegin rushed forward, searching the darkness. When he finally saw Janet on the ground, it was too late. She pulled the trigger and the first barrel spit fire, knocking Chief Keegin flat onto his back.

Among all the others who had followed from the dark depths of the cellar, Janet's mom screamed and ran toward him. "No!"

Janet fired the second barrel, hitting her mom in the thighs. She fell forward, face down, shrieking like a baby.

The shadows of the others backed away, staying near the burned house.

She dropped the gun and went to Facundo.

"Can you walk?"

He nodded.

Janet hooked a hand under his arm and helped him to his feet.

"She's dropped the gun!" her mom cried. "Get her!"

Janet looked at her mom as she crawled toward Chief Keegin's gun. The others, spurred by her words and obvious pain, moved closer, fanning out, trying to surround her.

"Come on! Let's move!"

Janet raced for the wall of brush as fast as she could with Facundo at her side. She was relieved when she saw the light of his trailer.

"Gabriel!" Facundo shouted.

The door opened and the boy ran out.

"¡Traiga a Dante!" Facundo said.

Gabriel ran back inside the trailer and returned a moment later with the Rottweiler.

"Dile que ataque," Facundo shouted.

"¿Her?" the boy asked.

"¡Ellos!" Facundo said and pointed to the people coming through the wall of brush. Gabriel unhooked the Rottweiler's leash and pushed him forward.

"¡Atacá!" Gabriel commanded, and the dog charged at high speed, barking. Soon the sound of ripping fabric was audible, even at a distance.

Gabriel ran back toward the trailer.

Janet saw a pick-up truck parked along the side of the trailer, covered with a tarp. "Does the truck run?"

"¿Qué?" Facundo said.

"Si," Gabriel replied. "Dame las llaves para el camión."

Facundo pulled keys out of his pocket and handed them to Janet.

In the orchard, someone screamed in pain. Then gunshots rang out and the Rottweiler stopped barking.

"¡Dante!" Gabriel cried.

"Hurry!" Janet said. "Please, Gabriel. Your dad needs you!"

Gabriel pulled the tarp off the truck.

Janet helped Facundo in on the passenger side, then climbed in behind the wheel.

Gabriel clambered into the bed and leaned through the open window in the back of the cab. He wiped tears from his eyes. "Let's go!"

Janet turned the key. The engine whined but didn't catch. "Oh, come on!"

Facundo reached over and pulled the choke. "Try it now."

"Right!" Janet turned the key again and the engine roared to life. She pushed the choke in and shifted into reverse. "Hang on!"

When she turned around, she saw Father Rozaro and some of the others closing in on the truck, their faces bathed in red from the brake lights. Janet gunned the engine. The tires threw dirt, and then the truck plowed through them in a cacophony of cracking bones and screams.

Janet spun the wheel, then shifted into drive, and sped toward the dirt road.

The steering wheel jerked back and forth as the truck bounced between the irrigation berms. She wouldn't slow down for anything. Not now. The truck roared out of the orchard and past the barn.

Janet swerved to avoid hitting the townsfolks' cars parked in and around the driveway. She plowed over the mailbox as she skidded off the driveway and onto the road.

Janet stomped the gas and the old truck shuddered as it picked up speed.

"¡Ve más despacio!" Facundo cried.

From the cab window, Gabriel said, "He says slow down."

"No!" Janet stared into the rear-view mirror, searching the darkness behind them for headlights. She didn't see the curve ahead.

"¡Estar atento!" Facundo said "¡Estar atento!"

"I'm not slowing down," Janet said.

"No, he says look out!"

Janet faced forward, seeing the curve, but too late to react. A tree loomed in the headlights, but just before the moment of impact, she managed to crank the wheel hard to her left. The tires shrieked and the truck rattled, but it remained on the road, missing the tree by inches. After another breakneck half minute, she eased off the gas, then slowed to a stop.

She was short of breath, her limbs weakened from the prolonged adrenaline. She looked over at Gabriel and Facundo. "How do you say 'sorry?' "

"Lo siento," Gabriel said.

"Lo siento, Facundo. Lo siento."

Facundo winced in pain, and Janet stepped on the gas.

5.

JANET SAT on the edge of a hospital bed. She had a bandage on her wrist. Brian stood next to her. She was lucky to have gotten through the last day relatively unscathed. She'd never felt like she'd had much luck in life, but that had certainly changed.

"Hello?" someone called out from the other side of the curtain.

"Yes?"

"It's Detective Kremler. Can I speak to you again?"

"Sure, detective."

He pulled open the curtain. His weathered face was grim.

"Well?" Brian said.

Kremler silently shifted the toothpick in his mouth from one side to the other.

"What is it?" Janet said.

"It's...unbelievable," Kremler replied. "No other word for it. Everything you've told us checks out."

Janet sighed, relieved and saddened at the same time. "Did you find Ethan?"

"In the morgue. Cause of death looks like blunt-force trauma."

"Oh, Ethan." Janet groaned and punched the bed. She felt like crying, but was all out of tears. Her first love, Joey's father, was dead. Her heart broke.

"Was it from the accident?" Brian asked.

"There was no accident. We found your car in Keegin's barn. Undamaged. They must have planned on staging it later."

"Like they did before," Janet said, sickened.

Kremler nodded.

"What about Angela?" Janet asked.

"She's still in surgery. I know she lost a lot of blood, but the doctor sounds positive. Same goes for Mr. Mardinez."

"And my mother?"

Kremler shook his head.

Brian patted her shoulder.

Janet knew she should feel sadness, but she only felt relief. She'd grieved the loss of her parents long ago. "What about the others?"

"Keegin was DOA. Everyone else from the scene was rounded up quickly. We caught Father Rozaro at the church. For some reason, he thought he had time to pack. Lucky for us. And if your father comes out of his coma, he'll be charged accordingly…" He paused. "For everything."

Janet said, "And Dr. Lawter?"

"Well…he did kill six people. He'd admitted to everything. But this ought to change things quite a bit. His case will have to be reopened at the very least because he was right. There really was a wide-ranging conspiracy involving a good number of locals."

"Jesus…" Brian whispered.

Kremler took the toothpick from his mouth. "First estimate from the coroner is that there are at least thirty sets of remains inside that pit under the house."

Brian covered his mouth, his face paling.

"As terrible as it is, a lot of people are going to finally get closure thanks to you."

"I shouldn't have let it get so far," Janet said. "I should have stayed. Made things right."

"You didn't know all of what was happening," Brian said. "At the time, you just knew you needed to get away. Who knows what might've happened if you didn't?"

Kremler patted her shoulder. "Me saying thank you isn't near enough, but…it'll have to do for now. Take care, okay?" He started to leave, then stopped at the curtain. "Oh. Almost forgot. There is one other thing. Turns out the Wozner boy was found last month, living with an uncle in Colorado."

"Are you sure?" Janet said in total disbelief.

The boy in the red jacket wasn't Ricky? Does that mean that…Joey?

"Yeah," Kremler said. "Why?"

Janet hesitated.

Brian squeezed her hand.

"It's…good news. That's all," she said, her throat tightening.

"Indeed, it is. Take care now." Kremler waved as he exited.

Shock stole over Janet. She was trying to process the information about Ricky, but was having trouble accepting it.

"Maybe it was Joey after all," Janet whispered. "The whole time, he could've been reaching out to me. Bringing me home. Bringing me here to find him."

Brian touched her chin, lifting her face to his. "It's over," he said. "That's all that matters. Right? That, and the baby."

Janet considered this for several seconds, then nodded. She didn't feel even the slightest hesitation. Not anymore. She wanted this baby, this life with Brian.

They hugged again, more tightly.

CEMETERY DANCE PUBLICATIONS
PAPERBACKS AND EBOOKS!

DEAR DIARY: RUN LIKE HELL
by James A. Moore

Sooner or later even the best prepared hitman is going to run out of bullets. Buddy Fisk has two new jobs, bring back a few stolen books of sorcery, and then stop the unkillable man who wants to see him dead…

"Gripping, horrific, and unique, James Moore continues to be a winner, whatever genre he's writing in. Well worth your time."
—Seanan McGuire, *New York Times* bestselling author of the *InCryptid* and *Toby Daye* series

DEVIL'S CREEK
by Todd Keisling

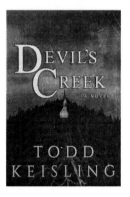

When his grandmother Imogene dies, Jack Tremly returns to his hometown to settle her estate. What he finds waiting for him are dark secrets which can no longer stay buried.

"Keisling skillfully evokes the landscape and inhabitants of south-central Kentucky, as well as the struggles of his protagonist to deal with a past resurgent in the most immediate and frightening ways. Another step forward for him, Devil's Creek *shows why Todd Keisling runs at the front of the pack."*
—John Langan, author of *Sefira and Other Betrayals*

HOLY GHOST ROAD
by John Mantooth

Some roads are haunted by the past. Some by ghosts. Some are even haunted by demons. The one Forest must travel is haunted by all three…

*"*Holy Ghost Road *is a southern fried coming-of-age road novel mashed with an epic good vs. evil yarn. Thrilling from page one, as well as inventive and compassionate, the book made me want to go climb the nearest tree and sit in the branches with Forest."*
—Paul Tremblay, author of *The Pallbearers Club*

Purchase these and other fine works of horror from Cemetery Dance Publications today!
www.cemeterydance.com